# To Hull And Back

Short Story Anthology 2018

# INTRODUCTION

Welcome to the fifth To Hull And Back short story anthology. I hope you enjoy all the ingenious sagas contained within this tremendous omnibus of amusing wonderment.

My competition 'reading, judging, deliberating and having a nightmare making a decision because the stories are all too good' trip was very enjoyable this year, but more challenging than ever – there were 100s of excellent stories entered into the competition, all exhibiting a wide range of qualities. The shortlisted stories contained in this book are the most superlative, weaved with care, skill and just a smattering of magic. Each author has the right to be prouder than a proud thing that is very proud indeed.

The anthology opens with the three winning stories of the 2018 competition. These are followed by the three highly commended tales from the runners-up, in alphabetical order (based on story title). After that, the other 14 shortlisted stories appear, again, in alphabetical order.

A story written by each of the judges closes the anthology. This is so future To Hull And Back competition entrants can see the types of stories the judges write and learn about their tastes. I hope this might give writers a better chance of penning a successful story for future competitions.

I'd like to express my utmost thanks to all the authors of the stories that appear in the 2018 anthology. It's an honour to be able to present them in this collection.

Chris Fielden

# CONTENTS

## JUDGE'S STORIES

# ACKNOWLEDGEMENTS

Thank you to Christie Cluett, Crystal Jeans, Edward Field, Mark Rutterford, Mel Ciavucco and Mike Scott Thomson for helping me judge the competition. Crystal and Mike are both previous To Hull And Back competition winners. Myself, Christie, Ed, Mark and Mel belong to a writing group in Bristol called Stokes Croft Writers:
www.christopherfielden.com/about/stokes-croft-writers-talking-tales.php

Thanks to Charlotte Strike for designing the cover of this book. You can learn more about Charlotte's artwork here: www.instagram.com/ca.strike/

Thanks to David Fielden for building and maintaining my website. Without him, I'd never have created a platform that allowed the greatest writing prize in the known macrocosm to have been conceived and launched. You can learn more about Dave's website services at: www.bluetree.co.uk

And finally, a HUGE thank you to everyone who entered the To Hull And Back contest this year. The volume of entries has enabled me to increase the prize fund for next year's competition for the fifth year running. Without the support of all those who entered, this just wouldn't be possible.

WINNING STORIES

# LIPS

*The winning story, by John Holland*

As they were leaving the college she asked him if he wanted a coffee. He said that he only drank tea. And walked on. The following week she asked him if he wanted a tea. In the café, they talked about the pottery class. She told him her name was Dorothy. Dorothy, he repeated. He didn't say his name, so she asked. He said it was Ellsworth.

After, he returned home to his small room with the skylight and the empty dog basket with the hair-matted maroon rug, and the small circular oak table with the vase-shaped stain. And sat in his uncomfortable wooden armed chair, picked up his ballpoint pen and opened his book – the one without the lines – and wrote the date (14th January 2006) and the word 'Tea'.

At the pottery class, he made a black iron-glazed stoneware urn which she admired. She made a blue-glazed earthenware plate with yellow and white-glazed fried eggs, orange-glazed beans and brown-glazed individually cut chips, which he didn't comment on.

After the class, Dorothy again invited Ellsworth for a tea. And when classes ceased they continued to meet in the café each month. He always drank tea. Occasionally they had a sandwich. Even at those prices.

After five teas in five months, they touched cheeks as they parted. His lips briefly on her skin. It felt strange to him. He liked it. He liked her, he thought. He didn't want to do anything sudden.

Back in his room he placed the metal end of a tape measure against the midpoint of his cheek. Then extended the tape to his lips. The centre, not the edge of his lips. Then removed it, holding the tape between his thumb and forefinger, and examined the numbers and lines on it. 100 millimetres or 10 centimetres. Her cheek and lips must be similar, he thought.

Using a blue plastic calculator, a piece of A4 paper from his book – the one with the lines – and a short, almost blunt, pencil, he began to draw up a grid. He calculated that if, when they parted each month, he moved his lips one millimetre towards her mouth he would reach her lips in eight years and four months. He had the time, he thought. He looked in his *Oxford*

*Pocket Dictionary*, eighth edition, 1992, and wrote the date in his book – the one without the lines – and the word 'incremental'. He sighed. Eight years and four months. He didn't want to do anything sudden.

The next time they met (June 2006) he felt slightly anxious, as he had to move his lips one millimetre towards hers. Because of his pre-occupation with this, he hardly talked at all. Only a few words about pulling handles on jugs. As they parted, he kissed her cheek in what he hoped was one millimetre closer to her lips. He couldn't be exactly sure. He couldn't really measure it, could he? She didn't seem to notice. In his room he wrote the date and the words 'Plan commenced'.

By January 2007 (eight months into his plan) his lips, he thought, had moved roughly eight millimetres towards her lips. He didn't think that she had noticed. He barely had.

When they met in the café in March 2007 (10 months/10mm) he talked about the Japanese potter, Hamada, and she talked about her husband. He said that he didn't know she had a husband. Didn't you notice my ring? she asked. No, he said. His name is Chip, short for Charles, she said. Like on the plate you made? he said. Yes, she laughed. In his room he wrote in his book the date and the word 'Chip'. It made him feel sad. And a bit hungry.

In May 2007 (one year/12mm) he asked her if, as well as a husband, she had a dog. No, she said. It's just that at home I have a basket, he said. Sorry, she said.

In September 2007 (one year four months/16mm) they talked about transfer-printed pottery and she told him that she dyed her hair. What, is it not really green? he asked. No, she said, and called him silly. He had been called silly before. But, for the first time, he liked it. Are your eyes really blue? he asked. Oh yes, although they used to be more blue, she said. When he returned to his room he wrote the date and the words 'Less blue'.

In July 2008 (two years two months/26mm) she told him that she had left her husband. Why? he asked. I don't like him, she said. Me neither, he said. But you haven't met him, she said. I'm just supposing, he said. She told him she was now living with her sister. Does she have a dog? he asked. No, she said.

In September 2009 (three years four months/40mm) they talked about glazes, including nuka, the oriental rice-based glaze. She told him she had met an Egyptian sculptor. He has dreadlocks, she said. Dreadlocks – very secure, he said.

In December 2009 (three years seven months/43mm) she told him that the Egyptian sculptor made his work from human faeces and blood. Human faeces and blood, he repeated. When they parted he checked her cheek before kissing it. In his room he wrote the date and the words 'Shit sculptor'.

In May 2010 (four years/48mm) she told him she had moved in with the Egyptian sculptor. He blinked and said nothing. Later he said he had a headache and stood and left without kissing her cheek. In his room, he regretted doing that.

In December 2010 (four years seven months/55mm) they talked about kick wheels and she told him she was pregnant. With a baby? he asked. Yes, she said. When he returned to his room he wrote the date and the word 'Baby' in bigger letters than usual.

In June 2011, back home in his room, he reviewed his plan. Over five years had elapsed. He believed he had moved his lips slightly more than 60 millimetres or six centimetres. He thought he was on target. He didn't want to do anything sudden.

In August 2011, about the time Dorothy was giving birth, a woman in the laundrette asked Ellsworth if he would like a coffee. Tea, he said, and felt proud of his assertiveness. In the café, he asked her name. Ernestine, she said. Ernestine, he repeated. And he told her his name, before chatting to her about clay and throwing and glazes and kilns. She seemed interested. As they parted he moved to kiss her cheek. Instead she kissed his lips. When he returned to his room he wrote the date and the words 'Spin cycle'.

The next month, September 2011, he met Ernestine again. At her suggestion he tried a cappuccino, but didn't like it. He brought with him a copy of *Ceramic Review* magazine which he leant her. He asked her if she ever threw pots. Only when I'm cross, she said. He didn't get it. He asked her if she was married. No, she said. Whether she dyed her hair. No, she said. Whether she knew anyone who made sculptures from human blood and faeces. No, she said. What's with all the questions? she asked. As they parted she kissed him again on the lips, and asked him if he wanted to see her room. Do you have a dog? he asked. No, she said. When he returned to his own room he wrote the date and the word 'No'. He regretted lending her the *Ceramic Review*.

In January 2012 (five years eight months/68mm) he met Dorothy again and this time she brought the baby. It was a boy. He asked his name. Donald, she said. Donald, he repeated. He asked if that was an Egyptian name. Not really, she said. When they parted he wasn't sure whether to kiss the baby on the cheek too. He didn't. But he did move his lips seven millimetres nearer her lips to compensate for the period when he hadn't seen her. He hoped that this was not too sudden and that she would not notice. As far as he knew, she didn't. Although he thought Donald might have.

In July 2012 (six years two months/74mm) Donald was with her again and cried and seemed unhappy. She said she had to go and change him. When she came back he was surprised. It's the same baby, he said. He's just pooed, she said. He asked if the baby's poo would be used for a sculpture. She said it wouldn't.

In February 2013 (six years nine months/81mm) she stopped bringing Donald with her. Her mother was looking after him, she said. They talked about Japanese anagama kilns. And she told him that she'd left the Egyptian sculptor. To come for a coffee? he asked. No, forever, she said. That's a long time, he said. Are you pleased? she asked. Yes, he said. She looked at him. He looked at her. He didn't want to do anything sudden. When he returned to his room he wrote the date and the word 'Forever'.

In December 2013 (seven years seven months/91mm) he talked to her about the best time to buy a new dog. How long since your dog died? she asked. He paused. His eyes moved upwards and to the right as he thought. I've never owned a dog, he said. Now might be a good time then, she said. When he returned to his room he wrote the date, and, in a rather shaky hand, the word 'Now'.

In August 2014 (eight years three months/99mm) he knew he was one millimetre from his target. From her lips. From kissing her. They talked about the porous qualities of unglazed earthenware. When he returned to his room he wrote the date and the words 'Rome wasn't built in eight years and four months'.

In September 2014 (eight years four

months/100mm) he knew he had reached his target date. He felt anxious. They talked about salt glazing and its impact on the environment. But he knew what he must ask himself to do. He tried to summon all the courage it had taken to hatch his plan, the courage he'd needed to try that cappuccino, the courage he'd shown by not going to Ernestine's room, the courage that had made him wait so long – so very long – for this woman. When they were about to part, he pressed his lips gently on hers.

That was sudden, she said.

When he returned home to his small room with the skylight and the empty dog basket with the hair-matted maroon rug, and the small circular oak table with the vase-shaped stain, he sat in his uncomfortable wooden armed chair, and picked up his pen and opened his book – the one without the lines – and wrote the date and the word 'Lips'. And then she wrote the word 'Lips' too.

~

# John Holland's Biography

John Holland is a prize-winning short fiction writer from Stroud in Gloucestershire in the UK. As well as winning and being short listed in contests, his work has appeared in many anthologies, magazines and online.

John likes to take his stories on the road and has read/performed in London, Bristol, Bath, Cheltenham (including at the Literature Festival), Worcester, Coleford, his home town of Stroud and, of course, Hawkesbury Upton. He prefers his audiences to be drunk.

His website is: www.johnhollandwrites.com

John is also the organiser of the twice-yearly live lit event Stroud Short Stories. The website is: www.stroudshortstories.blogspot.com

'Lips' was first published in *The Bath Short Story Award Anthology 2015*, after being longlisted in the competition.

~

## John Holland – Winner's Interview

1. What is the most interesting thing that's ever happened to you?

There are so many... Certainly, one of them was taking over the running of the twice-yearly Stroud Short Stories event here in Gloucestershire back in 2014. This means that much of my 'writing' time is spent supporting and promoting other writers. I enjoy that. (Some may say it's an excuse for me not to write.)

Also, in terms of interesting things, I once went to the toilet with the popular recording artist, Joe Jackson. He's bigger than you imagine. Tall, I mean.

2. Who is the most inspirational person you've ever met and why?

I'm lucky enough to have (briefly) met some of my heroes – Billy Wright, Ivor Cutler, John Cooper Clarke, Armando Iannucci, Harry Hill, Steve Bull, Dave Eggers, Margaret Atwood, Mike Gibbs, Jon Hiseman, Seb Rochford and not forgetting Joe Jackson.

The most inspirational of them? The late Ivor Cutler. He said, "You don't look like a fool to me."

3. Which authors do you most admire and why?

I love some short story writers and would like to be them.

Mainly, Jon McGregor, Etgar Keret, Alice Munro, Ivor Cutler, Richard Brautigan, Raymond Carver, Carson McCullers, J D Salinger, Thomas Morris and Angela Readman.

Their stories are either absurd or have heart. In the case of Cutler, both.

4. When and why did you start writing short stories?

I retired after 37 years as a librarian in 2010 when I was 58. I wanted to do something to keep my brain active so I went on a cookery course and a creative writing course. I had never written a short story before (although I wrote satirical gags for BBC Radio shows and *Punch* magazine in the 1980s).

I loved the cookery course. But the first story I wrote (literally, the first) was published by my tutor, Rona Laycock, so the old competitive side of me kicked in. I started entering competitions in 2013. For validation, I suppose. And then I was hooked. This is my fifth first prize in five years. And I've had about 80 pieces published in that time. Bonkers. I still don't really believe it. I don't particularly rate my own writing.

5. Where do your ideas and inspiration come from?

Songs (I have based stories on songs by The Band, the Arctic Monkeys and Billie Holiday), relationships, comedy, nature, my imagination and, very often, other people's short stories – see list above. There's something about Jon McGregor's writing that makes my brain explode with ideas.

I'm also inspired by the stories we receive for Stroud Short Stories, the event for local writers that I run. We receive 100 or more submissions each time. Some of the stories which make the final 10 are truly brilliant. The success of some of the SSS authors in the big wide world of short story competitions and publication seems to support my view.

6. Where do you write?

On the PC, in the back bedroom which is strewn with books, papers and LPs. It's a right mess. On holiday, I write long hand in books – ones both with and without lines.

7. How do you cope when your writing is rejected?

Traditionally, very badly indeed, but I've got used to it now. Many of my pieces, which were initially turned down, have gone on to find success elsewhere, so I'm more philosophical these days.

8. Who has published your work before?

InkTears, Dorset Fiction Award, Bath Short Story Award, Momaya Press, NFFD, NZFFD, Molotov Cocktail, The Cabinet of Head, Ellipsis Zine, Reflex Fiction, Worcs Literary Festival, Hawkesbury Upton LitFest, Earlyworks Press, Bangor Literary Journal, 101Words, Paragraph Planet, Raging Aardvark, Flash Fiction Magazine, Marble City Publishing, Stroud Short Stories (before I ran it) and, back in 2016, To Hull And Back. And, I dare say, others.

9. Why did you choose to enter the To Hull And Back competition?

Much of my writing might be termed humorous, or at least ironic, and To Hull And Back is that rare bird – a humorous short story comp.

It's also a fun comp. No one else puts your face on a motorbike or the cover of an anthology or meets you in Hull. For good reason.

There are some well-known comps that I no longer submit to. Chris Fielden of THAB seems to me to get it right. He tells you the time scale. He tells you the names of the judges. He tells you how many stories they will judge. He tells you when the results are in. He offers good prizes. He cares. And, of course, my story won. Smack on, Chris.

10. What will you spend your prize money on?

My mum died in 1992, so I thought I might buy a new one.

11. What has been your proudest writing moment so far?

I enjoy reading my stories (aloud) mostly in Gloucestershire, Bath and Bristol and love making audiences laugh.

Those words 'love making' look a bit odd there.

It's a huge fillip too, to win short story and flash fiction competitions, so I am immensely grateful to To Hull And Back, the Dorset Fiction Award, InkTears,

Momaya Press and the Worcs Literary Festival. Have you met Huge Fillip? Lovely guy. Smaller than you'd expect. Unlike Joe Jackson.

I'm pretty pleased with short listings, long listings, commendations and publications too. They're all cigars in my book. Oh, health and safety warning.

Some of my stuff is just so strange that I often think that those who publish it are going out on a bit of a limb. In a world in which so much short story/flash fiction writing is serious, sometimes over-serious, sometimes po-faced, I am really grateful to those folks who reward my efforts.

12. What advice would you give to novice writers?

I have lots of advice for novices.

The first is not to listen to anyone who gives you advice. At least be selective.

Just be yourself when you're writing. Don't try to conform to some mythical model of what others call 'good writing'.

Also you're never too old (or young) to start writing.

Read a lot, join a writing group where less than 50% of the members are a pain in the arse. And edit, edit, edit. Just keep editing your story.

I love something Tania Hershman said about stories promising the reader something at the beginning which they must fulfil by the end. Think about that.

And think particularly carefully about your story endings. One that's too overstated can ruin a story. When you've finished, take out the final sentence and see if the ending is better. Then take out the sentence before that and so on.

I did write a final piece of advice but I've taken it out.

# GRANDPA JOE STEPS OUT

*The second place story, by Aphra Pell*

The old man sat at the kitchen table, working on a crossword. He glanced up as I came in.

"Hello, Jo-jo. Was it a good party? Seven down. 'The flowering or royal fern.' Six letters. Second letter is 's'."

I froze, the door frame digging into my back.

"There's no need to look like a shocked goat. Don't you remember your old grandpa?"

I did. Of course I did. Grandpa Joe. My great grandpa, the source of childhood treats and sweets. I knew exactly who he was. The problem was I'd just come home from his wake.

*

I fled upstairs to the bathroom, bolting the door. I was leaning on the sink trying to control my breathing when I realised the shower curtain beside me was closed. Shaking slightly, I reached out my hand.

"'A hot air bath.' Ten letters. Ends in 'm'. Now, Jo-jo, are you going to run around like a weasel with its arse on fire or sit down and talk to me?"

He was in the tub, propped up with Aunt Cynthia's frilly pink bath pillow. Where his trouser legs hitched up, tartan sock suspenders peeked out. I subsided onto the closed toilet lid. It is hard to be terrified of an elderly man in tartan sock suspenders, even if you have been to his cremation.

"Good girl. How did the funeral go? Crematorium I suppose. I never liked the idea, but it turns out not to matter much."

"It... it was fine," I said. "Very nice. We had music... um..." Shaking, I pointed to a curl of black smoke that was rising from Grandpa Joe's left ear. He squinted sideways.

"Oh, don't worry about that, sweetheart. Normal side-effect. At least it's not beetles or worms, which is the downside of being buried. Henry VII has a terrible case of beetles apparently. Crawling in them."

"Henry...?" I stood up, felt faint, and sat down again abruptly. Grandpa Joe took this for acquiescence.

"Good girl. There's no point in running. If I am a figment of your imagination, you can't escape, and if I'm not, you wouldn't want to, would you? It's been years since we had a nice talk."

I nodded mutely. That was true. Grandpa Joe hadn't held a coherent conversation for 10 years. He put down the magazine and looked at me across the top of his glasses. I remembered that look.

"Now. I am, as you can see, a ghost of sorts. It turns out all those silly paranormal people were correct, which is very irritating. When people die, some pass on, and some get stuck. I'm stuck, and I think I know why."

I watched as more smoke spiralled up from his ear. A faint smell of cold ashes tainted the room. I took a deep breath.

"OK, I'll play along. And can you call me Jo please? No one has called me Jo-jo since..." Since Grandpa Joe had his first stroke. "Never mind, Jo-jo is fine. Why are you stuck?"

Grandpa Joe looked at his old-fashioned watch.

"Your aunt should be asleep by now. Best not to involve her I think. Get my box, and then you and I can go for a little drive."

*

Grandpa Joe's box was the family reliquary. Inside was the debris of the twentieth century: ration books, newspaper cuttings, Nana Anna's pair of celluloid hair combs, complete with rhinestones. To me it had the vintage romance of a black and white movie. I pulled it out of the sideboard and took it outside to my car.

"Put it in the footwell, sweetheart. I'm not sure I'm solid enough to have it on my lap, and no one wants a couple of pounds of pine in their bowels. Find a map on that phone thingy of yours, and we'll get going."

"It's nearly midnight."

"Which means we'll be there before dawn. Fewer

questions, Miss Nosey Parker, and more driving please. The sooner we get there, the sooner you'll know. And it is important you know, I think. It's important that someone knows before I'm gone."

*

"That's £34.90 for the petrol. Those too?"

The cashier scanned the tin of boiled sweets while I watched Grandpa Joe in the car. In the artificial light of the service station forecourt he had a slight transparency. It didn't seem to be stopping him from fiddling with my phone.

"Tap or insert your card please."

Grandpa Joe. My only grandfather really. Mum's parents died years ago. Dad's live in Spain. It was Grandpa Joe who took us out every Sunday, to his allotment or to feed the ducks, then brought us home for one of Aunt Cynthia's 'proper' teas. It was Grandpa Joe who had been there for us. Until that day 10 years ago when the phone rang, and Mum dashed out of the house, telling me to make my brother breakfast and refusing to say why. I made frosted cereal. I haven't eaten it since.

"Oooh, sucky sweeties. We always had these when I took you to the seaside, do you remember?" Grandpa Joe fumbled my phone back into the holder and edged the tin out of my hands. I took it back and yanked the lid off for him, noting he had somehow cracked my phone's password and flipped through my photos.

"I wouldn't dream of making a trip without them, Grandpa."

Ghosts can suck boiled sweets. They do it noisily.

\*

Our destination was a graveyard, in a town 100 miles away. The church, a great Victorian gothic shadow, loomed out of the pre-dawn grey among sprawling yews. I sat down on a dew dampened bench with the sacred box on my knees. Grandpa was poking at a nearby grave with his foot.

"Hah. George Wranby. He was landlord of the Lion when I was stationed here. A bigger black marketeer you'd have to go to London to find. Always talked big about what he'd do after the war." He peered more closely at the gravestone. "Died 28th November 1945. Poor chap. It's not fair really." He went faint and then reappeared at my side. "Here we are then."

"Yes." I said. "Here we are. Are you going to tell me why?"

"All in good time, Jo-jo. You're always rushing." He gazed out across the dim yard. "You made time to come and see me though. I appreciated that, even if I couldn't show it."

I dug in my pocket for another sweet. The stroke hadn't killed Grandpa Joe. He'd been 88, with no right to survive, but survive he had. Or someone had. An old man who staggered with assistance, ate with assistance, and scowled at his carers, even if he couldn't remember their names. I'd visited every week, but it wasn't Grandpa Joe I'd sat with, watching telly in that nursing home room.

I felt a light touch against my cheek and laughed, swallowing tears as rubbery fingers pinched my nose. Whether I was hallucinating or haunted, this man *was* Grandpa Joe.

We sat in silence as the sky lightened and started to

colour with dawn. I yawned. The whole night was catching up with me.

"You should get some kip before you drive back, sweetheart, we don't want another funeral." He paused. "I'm not coming back with you. This is where I need to be."

I looked round at the unfamiliar church in the unfamiliar town.

"Why? You haven't lived here for over 70 years."

"I know," Grandpa Joe said. "Just a few short years a lifetime ago. But this is where I need to be." He took a deep breath, in so far as a ghost can. "You see, this is where I fell in love."

*

I don't remember Great-nana Anna, but I know the story. She and Grandpa Joe were childhood sweethearts, posted apart in war, reuniting to marry at combat's end. It was family truth. Apparently it was family lie.

"I can guess what you are thinking, Jo-jo. But it wasn't like that. Your nana and I... we grew up together, got in trouble together, she was my best friend. But we never courted."

"Then why did you marry her?"

"Because the war came. Because in war, a lot of rules get broken, and no one is to blame." He smiled at me, a little sadly.

"Don't judge us. Anna fell in love while she was away, just like I did, and the war made things more urgent for us all. Unfortunately, the man she fell in love with had a wife safely at home, a little thing he neglected to mention until several mornings after. That left Anna in a bit of a pickle when the doctor diagnosed twins."

"You took the blame and saved her?"

"Not blame, sweetheart. Not saved either, your nana never needed rescuing. She chose with her eyes open. I asked for the privilege of being her husband and a father, and I was a husband and a father. Cynthia and your grandad, your mum and her brothers, and you and your brother, you are all mine. Nothing changes that."

We sat in silence again. I could hear the traffic on the road behind, but in front only an early visitor at the far side of the graveyard broke the dead peace.

"Wasn't it unfair though? On the woman you fell in love with? Or was she married too?"

Grandpa Joe was looking straight ahead, his face seeming far younger. He looked now like the moustachioed middle-aged man in flares and long-collared shirts who had pride of place on Mum's mantelpiece. I could see tears brimming in his eyes. Too late to take the question back. I thought of another reason for being free to marry.

"Oh. I'm sorry, Grandpa. I didn't..."

He waved a hand at me.

"Don't apologise, Jo-jo. Yes. They died." He swallowed. "That's why marrying your nana was so easy. I knew I'd not find a woman I liked better. To have a best friend and a family... it seemed more than I deserved."

"I'm sorry. Are they buried here?"

"Yes."

"And you need to find their grave? Visit it or something?"

"Perhaps. But..." His voice shook. "I think... I think maybe they have found me." He rubbed at his eyes as the tears spilled over.

I followed his gaze. The figure I had taken to be another visitor was standing between two yews. Immaculate in World War II pilot's kit, he was smiling at us.

*

"Do stop blaspheming, Jo-jo, and open the box. I need that." Grandpa Joe jabbed a finger at a small cardboard box lodged in one corner. It was the only thing amongst all the mementos that I was not allowed to touch. I'd taken it out once. Grandpa Joe hadn't been angry, not the nasty shouting sort, he never was. But I'd never touched it again.

I opened it now. A warm gold signet ring sat amongst ancient cotton wool. Grandpa Joe stood up and then sat down again, as indecisive as a schoolboy on his first date. He took my hands in his spongey grasp and held them on his knee.

"Listen, Jo-jo. You need to know this." He swallowed again, looking down at our clasped hands, at the ring held between my fingers. "He gave me that."

I glanced up at the man between the yews. He was watching us patiently.

"On the last day I saw him. He kissed me, on the way back to base in the dark of the blackout where no one could see us. And I kissed him, and I meant it and wanted it, I'd wanted it since the day we met. And... your nana wasn't the only one who broke the rules. The next day, he slipped that ring into my hand."

Tears, hot, damp and real, fell on my fingers.

"And I, coward that I was, gave it back and ran away. I had a few days leave due, and I ran away to cower."

Blue eyes, young, urgent blue eyes now, met mine. "I was ashamed you see. Ashamed for what I was, and ashamed of my shame. While I was hiding from myself at home, he came limping back to base in a wounded plane that crashed 50 yards from the runway."

"I'm sorry." It sounded feeble, but I couldn't think what else to say. Grandpa Joe, having got the worst of it out, continued in a calmer tone.

"I don't know what I'd have done if he'd lived. I like to fool myself that I'd have been strong, honest, but who knows. Maybe I would have married Anna anyway, lived an even bigger lie. The Germans made sure I never had to decide. I came back from leave to be met by a box of personal effects and the news that I, his so-called best friend, his traitor, was the beneficiary of the will. It only amounted to some books and a bank account with £3, 11s in it, but there in the bottom of the box, under his shirts and socks, was that ring. I knew I had to keep it." Grandpa Joe reached out his hand, fumbling with the band. I caught it and slipped it on his finger.

The young man between the trees leant against an overwrought angel and puffed on his pipe. He looked like he had all the time in the world. I wiped my eyes with the back of my hand.

"You'd better go and join him then," I said. "You've kept the poor guy waiting long enough."

Grandpa Joe stood up, straighter and taller than I ever remembered him.

"You haven't asked why I asked you to come here, Jo-jo."

"Well... I assume I'm your favourite."

He laughed.

"You are, sweetheart, you always were. But that's not the reason. I looked at that telephone thingy of yours. Those things are surprisingly easy to use when you're dead."

"I saw. You went sneaking through my photos. But..."

He looked at me.

"Take her home to meet your mum, Jo. Don't be a coward. Don't be a fool and wait 70 years. You don't need to."

I nodded, feeling the prickle behind my eyes again. Grandpa Joe leant down and pinched my nose one last time, then turned and walked towards the yews and the young pilot with the pipe. His clothes started to change, from his favourite old tweeds to a flight suit and bomber jacket. I looked away, down at poor ambitious George Wranby's grave.

*

Three hours later, I'm sitting in a service station café, necking strong coffee and staring at my phone. I know who I need to call and what to say. I'll say it in memory of Grandpa Joe.

~

## Aphra Pell's Biography

Aphra was born slightly too long ago in the UK, in a dilapidated cottage with dogs and cats, and a lot of books. She now lives in Australia in a disorganised bungalow, with a husband and a large number of rats. There are still a lot of books.

Aphra splits her time between science academia, writing for clients and writing fiction. Day jobs include teaching palaeontology and writing ad copy for romance novels. Despite these qualifications she has yet to produce any dinosaur erotica.

You can find out more about her writing at www.aphrapell.com or follow her on Twitter @AphraPell for a large number of posts about small furry animals, large furry animals, and animals that aren't furry at all.

# THE PIG

*The third place story, by Pat Winslow*

The pig was dead. How it got there, we never found out. It was lying on its side on the front doorstep like a slab of concrete. If you kicked it, the flesh didn't wobble.

"It's rigor mortis," I told my mother.

"Rigor nothing," she said. "The pig's got to go."

But we couldn't shift it. We asked our neighbour to help. He couldn't shift it either. He phoned his son and told him to come from work.

"He's got a pick-up truck," he said. "With a winch."

We attached the pig to it. The winch broke.

The pig stayed there all day. It started to rain. You could see it reflected in the puddle. *Now we've got two pigs*, I thought. My mother made scrambled eggs on toast. We hadn't eaten all day. We were ravenous.

A policeman came. *That's three now*, I thought. But I didn't say anything.

"What's this?" he said.

"What does it look like?" I said. "It's a pig."

"Are you trying to be funny?" he said.

"No," I said. "We just found it. Somebody put it there this morning."

"Who?" said the policeman.

"If I knew, I'd ask them to take it away," I said.

The policeman drove off.

That night the rain got heavier. The pig was starting to look different. It looked sort of floppy. I touched its ear with my foot. It moved. Definitely floppy. It was starting to decompose.

"That's the next stage," I told my mother. "We can chop it up now and put it in the bin. Get rid of it that way."

But we didn't because it was still raining and the streetlight wasn't working properly so we wouldn't have been able to see what we were doing anyway.

"We'll leave it 'til tomorrow," I said.

The next morning there was a man from the council and two policemen came this time.

"Have you noticed they're not sending any women here?" I said to my mother.

She was too busy making tea to notice. She was laying out biscuits in a fan shape on the plate.

"We've got plenty more," she said as she handed them around.

The policemen took two each. When they thought I

wasn't looking, they took two more. The man from the council took one. He was thin and whiskery and spoke with an accent.

"Where are you from?" my mother asked him.

He just looked at her and said nothing. There was a crumb on his tie. I wanted him to brush it off. I couldn't stop looking at it.

"This pig," he said at last. "You know it's a health hazard?"

"We've had complaints," said one of the policemen. "I have to ask you to move it."

"Or get a licence," said the other one. "You need a licence to keep a pig."

"It's dead," I said.

"More tea?" said my mother.

They held out their cups.

"Is this the hacksaw you propose to use?" the council official said when we told him our plan.

"It is."

"You've tried cutting up a pig before?"

"Never."

"Then I don't think it'll work," he replied.

"And," said the policeman who knew all about pigs, "the bin isn't a good idea."

I could see his point. The pig was crawling with blowflies. They were laying eggs everywhere.

"We'll send someone round," said the whiskery man from the council. "Someone with a truck and a winch."

Before it went dark a man with a notebook came to inspect the site. He took a tape measure out of his pocket and began sizing up the space outside our front door.

"For the truck," he said.

He ate two lemon puffs and a French fancy. My

mother had sent me out at lunch time to replenish our stocks.

"Men get hungry," she explained.

The truck arrived at 07:30 the next morning.

"That's early," my mother said. "They must be keen."

She went into the kitchen to put the kettle on.

The milkman came and went and the truck backed in slowly and swung out again and backed in and swung out and backed in and swung out.

"He's having trouble parking," said my mother. "Have you noticed how it's men they keep sending?"

After the 13th attempt, the driver thumped the steering wheel and yanked on the handbrake.

"Don't any of you lot go out to ruddy work?" he yelled out of his window. His face was purple and puffy.

"What do you mean?" My mother was bristling.

He pointed to the parked vehicles in our street, which wasn't strictly fair. It was on account of the pig that the neighbour's son's truck was still there with its broken winch. And I was planning to get my car off the blocks as soon as I could get new wheels and an exhaust for it. In fact, I'd been going to do that the day the pig arrived.

The driver sloped off to get some change so he could use the phone box down the bottom of our road. His mobile had run out of juice and we wouldn't let him use ours.

"I can't believe he's just left the truck here," my mother said. "At an angle. How's anyone supposed to get up and down our road now? Supposing there was a fire?"

Which there had to be, of course. It was only a minor fire, but you know what the fire brigade's like. They have to investigate everything and make sure it's safe. It was only toast and Mrs Haslam had put it out before they came. She'd even made a fresh batch. She was eating it when they turned into our road. The fire engine had to mount the pavement on the opposite side to get past. They hit the truck's wing mirror and tore it straight off. When the driver came back from the phone box he went ballistic.

"I'll have to go back to the depot now," he said. He turned to me and jabbed a finger in my chest. "Why didn't you tell me there was no phone in the bloody phone box?"

"How was I to know?" I said. "I never use it."

When he'd gone my mother gave the fire brigade some tea.

"We're running out," she whispered to me. "You'll have to buy some more."

*PG Tips are doing alright out of this pig*, I thought.

The policeman who knew all about pigs came back that evening to see how we were doing. We had the local newspaper there as well, taking pictures and asking questions.

"How long before the maggots hatch?" asked the journalist. He was a friendly looking chap.

"Why?" I asked.

"My brother goes fishing."

"There's carp in the canal now," said the policemen who knew all about pigs. It seemed there wasn't an animal he didn't know about because the conversation turned to sea bass and Portuguese man o' wars.

"What's one of those?" my mother asked.

"Jelly fish," he said. "Deadly. I know a man who had to have a leg amputated because of one."

"At least we don't have that lying on our doorstep,"

she said.

The next day was Sunday and no self-respecting council worker works on a Sunday so the pig stayed where it was. I was getting rather fond of it. There's a lot to watch in a decomposing pig. If the weather's right, the maggots hatch on the fourth day, which they did. I phoned the journalist and his brother came down straight away. He was picky though.

"They're not mature," he said. "Another few days and they'll be nice and plump. I'll come back then. If the pig's not gone, of course."

The pig wasn't gone. There was a strike. By the end of the week there were bin liners down our road as well as parked cars and a broken truck. The journalist came back.

"Have you got rats yet?"

I didn't like to ask what his brother wanted those for.

My mother made him a cup of tea and gave him a jam doughnut. He held the doughnut up and grinned at us.

"They call these Berliners in Germany. When John F Kennedy said, 'Ich Bin ein Berliner,' he was really saying, 'I'm a jam doughnut.'"

"I liked him," said my mother. "They shouldn't have shot him."

"The Germans?" I said.

For some reason the journalist thought this was very funny.

After a while, the pig began looking like a giant bruised thumb. It was swollen and black. The kids loved it. I had to stand guard over it so they didn't start poking and prodding it.

"A good thing we didn't put it in the bin," said my mother as she tied up another plastic bag full of rubbish and threw it in the road.

The day the strike ended, the pig changed colour again. It was sort of creamy now and wrinkled. It was caving in. My mother said it reminded her of her grandmother. I said I didn't think that was a nice thing to say.

"I know," she said. "But it's true."

The bin men were beeping and backing down our street with their lights flashing. There were two blokes walking down the other side of the road with rubber gloves slinging people's bin bags into the back. My mother gave them the thumbs up sign. They'd got their pay increase.

"It's still not enough," I said. "I wouldn't do their job."

We watched them working their way down the road. When they drove back up again, she asked them if they wanted a cup of tea.

"Can't stop," the bloke on our side said. "We said we'd get this backlog cleared by Wednesday. I see you've still got that pig."

"Yes," she said.

We were famous. We'd been in all the papers and *Look North* had come to do an interview.

"I saw you on the telly," the bin man said. "'I know her,' I said to my wife. 'I empty her bin.'" He walked over to the pig and touched it with the end of his boot. "It looks like my granddad, does that. I could weep. It's where we all end up, isn't it? Makes you think." He looked at me. "Let me know if you want any help shifting it," he said.

That afternoon we phoned the council.

"Any longer and you won't be able to pick it up with a winch," I told them. "It'll start fermenting and going mouldy. It'll be like beer with fluff and bits of bone in it."

The hair was already falling off and the ears had gone completely dry. There was a distinctly cheesy smell starting to come from it. It was worse than feet. Even the kids stayed away.

They sent a fork lift truck driver round.

"If they'd sent you in the first place, we'd have been back to normal," my mother said.

She was wrong. He took one look at the pig and fell over in a dead faint.

"Weak tea, that's what he needs," I said.

My mother pushed me out of the way.

"Get him a chair," she said. "And a glass of cold water."

If you've ever tried getting a chair and a glass of water past a pig on a doorstep you'll know how difficult it is. It didn't help that my laces were undone. I fell. My knees went into the pig's stomach cavity and the chair splintered underneath me and the water went everywhere. Miraculously, the glass didn't smash.

"Well, that's one thing," said my mother.

The man with the fork lift fainted again when I stood up and he saw my jeans. My mother called the council and said he wasn't fit. Let me speak to him, the council said. There must have been a difference of opinion because in the end his boss came round in a flash white car and told him to go home. He didn't give him a lift. He just drove off and left him there sitting on the pavement drinking water. Eventually, the bloke got in the fork lift and drove off.

"I don't think we're ever going to get rid of this pig," my mother said.

It wasn't so bad once the flies had gone and the

cheesy smell stopped being cheesy. There were lots of interesting beetles now and wasps and wispy grey fuzz.

"When it's bones we can throw it away like we were going to do," I said.

Once or twice we had art students coming to take photos of it. There was one with long hair who had a sketch book. On the last day she turned up with a folding chair and a box of paints and an easel. When she'd finished her painting she wrote 'death is beautiful' underneath it. She had funny green eyes with pupils that were the size of full stops. When she looked at me, they made me feel small and important at the same time.

"You make me feel like a microbe," I told her.

She smelt like wet earth. I wanted to be near her and away from her.

My mother could see what was happening from the window. It wasn't a tea and biscuit situation, she would tell me later.

The student asked me to bag up the bones for her. I took a shovel from our shed at the back and found a piece of hardboard to scoop them onto.

"Do you want me to wash them?" I asked her.

"That would be nice," she said.

My mother disappeared behind the curtains.

"Would bleach be a good idea?"

"That would make sense."

I asked Mrs Haslam if I could borrow her old galvanised iron tub. When I told her what it was for she said we could keep it.

It took quite a bit of time. We had to be careful. The art student helped me scrub the doorstep after we'd bagged everything up. It was the least she could do, she said. I watched her hair in the evening sun. It was swinging in swags. *Nothing will ever be the same after this*, I thought.

She looked up at me suddenly.

"You'll miss that pig, won't you?"

"Only a bit," I said. "It's like I grew up with it."

Which was a funny thing to say, because I was 29.

~

# Pat Winslow's Biography

Pat Winslow has had seven poetry collections published, most recently *Kissing Bones*, *Unpredictable Geometry* and *Dreaming of Walls Repeating Themselves* all with Templar Poetry. Her short fiction has appeared in anthologies and magazines and she is currently exploring the possibility of writing a libretto for an opera.

Further information is available on:

www.patwinslow.com

Pat also blogs at:

www.thepatwinslow.blogspot.co.uk

# HIGHLY COMMENDED STORIES

# FASHION IN MEN'S FOOTWEAR – LATE 20TH CENTURY

*Highly commended story, by Steven John*

The 1960's. With a shilling I can buy a stripy paper bag of lemon and lime chews. I watch the fat lady tip the sugary lipped jar over the pan on the scales. I scrutinise whilst she adds and subtracts sweets with her liquorice allsorts spade, until the big-hand points to four ounces-o-clock.

Outside, on her bicycle leant on the shop window, Pamela Blackwell has been holding my bike upright, her bare legs resting on her handlebars. I'd seen her red knickers as she pulled up her knees, so I squat down and re-tie the laces on my new black baseball boots.

On the path that leads to the woods I can't keep up with her. I breathe only the dust from her sherbet hair in the peppermint light that ripples through the leaves.

"If you give me all the red ones you can kiss me," she laughs out of sight.

I think, *for a shilling I could have bought a ton of strawberry hearts*.

"There aren't any red ones," I yell through tears, and wish that she'd notice my new black baseball boots.

I should be in the lead. I should be the one who decides what colour kisses are.

*

The 1970's. If I slide the driver's seat back as far as it can go, I can depress the clutch in my brown and cream, six-inch stacked platform shoes, although I can't feel if my right foot is on the miniscule brake or accelerator pedal.

Linda Osborne will be finishing her shift in the hotel restaurant at two-o-clock, just enough time for a pint in the bar. In her staff accommodation attic bedroom I unzip her out of her black waitress's skirt and unbutton her ironed white shirt. Her underwear smells of Sunday lunches.

"You're quite a bit shorter out of your shoes," she says on her narrow bed.

Linda knows where there's a party. I double de-clutch the car through the lanes whilst I stroke the inside of her thigh. The right hand bend is 30 degrees too many. My stacked right foot presses on the accelerator rather than the brake. A ditch and a dry-stone wall come between us and the party.

"You fucking idiot, you nearly killed me," she says

before pulling down her denim skirt and climbing up the ditch to the road.

"Well I've broken a heel," I tell her, "and they cost 30 quid."

The hotel chef arrives on his motorbike and helps Linda onto the pillion. I stand on my one good shoe so I'm as tall as he is.

\*

The 1980's. In the gentlemen's outfitters in Oxford, where university students of philosophy purchase their English mustard corduroy trousers, I buy black Oxford shoes with loops of perforations around the shiny toe-caps. I've got a diploma in business studies from the polytechnic, but in London's square mile we're all high flyers.

In the gentlemen's club in Soho we're measured up for girls and taxis hailed back to the company flat off Marble Arch. The fridge is stocked only with champagne. The boys take glasses and a bottle each then peel off to the bedrooms where the girls peel off for their share of the bonuses.

But I can't go to the bedroom. I've fallen in love with Mandy who kisses me on the ear so softly, her hair as sheer and as black as her stockings. She tells me she's from Jamaica, and only does this work because her banker husband left her with two young kids, and there's the mortgage and the private school fees to pay, and the nanny when they're not boarding away. I start to make plans for when she and her children move in with me, and I help her find a proper job, and we have two sweet, light brown kids of our own.

"Lover, are we going to do it or not?" she asks in the

kitchen, after the champagne and the talk has dried up.

"No," I say, "I respect you too much for that," and "can we meet outside of work any time soon, somewhere non-business related, as it were?"

"After work next Monday," she says, "but I need something to make up for lost income tonight."

I give her a hundred and open the cab door for her in the sober London dawn.

"You're a proper gentleman," she says and kisses me.

I look down at my black Oxfords. *Yes*, I think, *I am*.

"We haven't got any Jamaican Mandys here. Never had," says the doorman of the gentlemen's club on the Monday night.

I tip the shoeshine boy a fiver and buy new laces I don't need.

*

The 1990's. The sun boils into the beach buggy my fiancée Alison and I have hired for the day. I drive in bare feet even though the foot pedals are too hot to touch.

We drive through villages where children's faces watch our passing from glassless windows and baking stoops. Down a track that leads through breadfruit and banyan trees, the children run after us, shoeless over the sharp road-stone. White sand arcs round the green water and black shadows of coral. We leave the buggy in the shade of eucalyptus and take beach bags.

We lay our hotel towels under coconut trees and walk the length of the beach, hand in hand. I stop and throw fallen coconuts into the waves. We watch them bobbing like swimmers heads and wait for them to roll back up the sand. We've brought a picnic of wine and pink melons. I cut the melons with a knife borrowed from the hotel's buffet. I try to stab drinking holes in a coconut but miss and stab a hole in her towel.

"I hope I don't get stranded on a desert island with you," Alison says.

"We should go for a swim now we're here," I say, "skinny dipping. We're the only ones on the beach."

"No way," she says and asks me to hold her towel whilst she pulls on a one-piece.

"Reminds me of family holidays in Newquay," I say.

She won't go into the sea.

"It's too coral-ly and I didn't bring shoes."

Alison goes back into the shade and rubs in more high-factor. I do breaststroke over the warm swell. Two local girls come onto the beach and strip off at the water's edge. Under dirty dresses they're wearing bikinis but they toss the tops aside then high step over the waves. In the deeper water they arch their bodies then disappear under, their bottoms floating momentarily on the surface. I go back to the towels and stretch out. She's pretending to be asleep behind sunglasses. I close my eyes and listen to the two girls chattering like the frantic little birds in the papaya trees.

Then there's a heavy wet slap on my stomach. I don't look up.

"Ouch, what the hell was that for?"

"What was what for?" Alison says.

I look up. There's a lizard on me, rat sized, but with a longer tail. It's fallen, or jumped, from the coconut tree leaning over us. It turns its head to one side and winks at me.

"FUCKING HELL." I jump to my feet, flaying at my stomach. The back of my hand touches the lizard's mouth.

"Arrgh, I felt its flicky tongue."

Alison starts to laugh. I haven't seen her laugh since we arrived. I'm not sure I have ever seen Alison laugh like she is now.

"Serves you right. Those girls felt your 'flicky tongue' when you swam up close."

The lizard slinks into the undergrowth. I watch the girls skip out of the water and dress. They don't have towels but the water evaporates from their brown skin. When they walk past us, they're dry as pebbles.

"We should make love now we're here," I say to Alison, "deserted tropical beach, coconut trees…"

"And have a reptile crawl over me? No thanks."

We don't speak on the walk back to the buggy. Alison strides in front of me with her towel wrapped from her chest down. The top of the dashboard, behind the steering wheel, has been adorned with red and pink seashells and blooms of wild hibiscus.

"Gifts from the children," I say, and pull my camera from the beach bag.

"Put a flower behind your ear. Take the towel off. Let me take a photo."

She picks a compact mirror from her bag and smears sun block on her nose.

"Save it for the local fauna," she says.

One by one, my fiancée drops the seashells and hibiscus flowers into our slipstream. I stop at a roadside shack that has beach things for sale on a wooden trestle.

"I'm going to buy a pair of jelly shoes," I say. "I'm getting cold feet."

She raises her sunglasses. "Jelly shoes?

"Jelly shoes," she says, "are for wankers."

~

# Steven John's Biography

Steven lives in The Cotswolds, UK, and writes flash, short stories and poetry. He's had work published in pamphlets and online magazines including *Riggwelter, Reflex Fiction, Fictive Dream, Cabinet of Heed* and *Former Cactus.* In 2017 Steve won the inaugural Farnham Short Story Competition and has won Bath Ad Hoc five times.

Steve has read at Cheltenham Poetry Festival, Stroud Short Stories, Bard of Hawkwood and Flasher's Club.

Twitter: @StevenJohnWrite

# SEEDS

*Highly commended story, by Gaynor Jones*

Miss Williams had planned for everything, except the plants.

*

September. Miss Williams, like her new classroom, is primed and ready. As she checks the seating arrangements one final time, the hand-over chat from the previous teacher, Mrs Brannigan, rattles through her ears.

"That girl does nowt but whine. For Christ's sake, don't sit her near the front or yer ears will be bleedin' by three o'clock.

"You'll want soft lad there right at the back, near the window; some serious B.O. with that one.

"That bossy little gobshite will want to do all the jobs for yer so stick him over there, near the door where he can bob in and out. And give 'im some pencils to sharpen if he really starts gettin' on yer tits."

Miss Williams instead arranges the seating plan based on a balanced mix of friendship groups and last year's test results. She believes that this will work out just fine.

She strolls around her new classroom, breathing in the space. As she passes, she places a hand written note with a gender neutral superhero sticker and an alliterative welcome (*Brilliant to teach you, Briyah – Happy to meet you, Harry*) on top of each desk, to ensure all of the children will know their place and feel welcome when they arrive. She takes a moment to run her hands over the smooth surface of one of the desks. They are exquisite. Relics from the early years of the school that she has spent a whole summer sanding and polishing in her secluded yard, with only the occasional bee for company. The head teacher had wanted to throw them out, but Miss Williams had insisted. Such good workmanship. Open and close lids. Sturdy legs. Pot holes from the time of ink and feathers. She loves the idea of history in the present.

Miss Williams straightens her tweed trousers and re-ties the bow on her pussy-neck blouse. It's a bold choice of outfit for her, a crisp daffodil yellow chiffon that matches her display boards perfectly. This term's reading book is *The Secret Garden* and she has grand plans for these boards, a brown felt soil patch, reams of toilet roll tube stems and a burst of tissue paper blooms that her pupils will create with smiles on their faces.

Before the bell rings, Miss Williams reaches into a cardboard tube to remove and unfurl her pièce de résistance. It's a poster with a photograph of a tall oak tree and the words 'Teachers plant the seeds of knowledge that grow forever' written across the bottom in beautiful calligraphy. She tapes it to the inside of the classroom door, where the children will see it as they exit the classroom at the end of every day.

*

"No, Jacinta, you may not go to the toilet again.

"Yes, Teddy, you may get a ruler from the cupboard.

"Beautiful work, Carla. Here, have another sticker."

Miss Williams paces around the room, alert for any sign of rebellion. A turned head. A dropped pencil. A whispered slur. She bobs up and down, leans in, hovers over, pats arms, answers questions, asks questions and hands out sticker after sticker after sticker. It is exhausting. *Exhausting.* It's nothing to do with the things she was warned about – the planning and the meetings and the marking, she is handling all of that fine. It's the children. Nobody really warned her about the children.

They.

Do.

Not.

Stop.

Talking.

Miss Williams does sometimes think, but only sometimes, about placing the stickers on their mouths instead of their jumpers or charts. How much quieter fidgety little Paul would be with several 'good job' smiley faces slapped on his chocolate-milk-spattered mouth. But then, that strategy wouldn't work out anyway, because – in strict accordance with her thoroughly researched behaviour management scheme – only the well behaved pupils are getting stickers. The ones who are quiet and studious and working and always doing the right thing. Because she has been told, by all of the lecturers on her training course and all of the books piled in her study, that if she rewards the well behaved pupils often enough and loud enough and merrily enough then the others will follow suit. But unfortunately this, as Miss Williams is beginning to painfully discover, is utter bollocks.

"Miss Williams?"

It's Jacinta again.

"Yes?"

"There's a weird green thing in my desk."

Everybody turns then. Of course they do. Miss Williams strides over, barely containing her flush.

"Eyes front, children. Let's see who can get a super copying sticker to add to their chart." On the way to the back of the classroom, she doles out gold stars to any child who has turned around to face the board again.

"Did you put this here, Jacinta?"

It is a plant. Plain as day. A small, green stem with a dainty cluster of yellow-centred flowers at the top. Miss Williams crouches down until she is eye level with it.

"No, Miss. I just seen it now."

"*Saw* it."

Miss Williams considers the plant. Maybe a crack in

the wood? A seed blown in on the breeze? She reaches into her pocket, wraps her nude manicured finger tips around a tissue, pinches the tissue around the stem, plucks the stem from the desk, then tosses the lot in the bin before any more disruption can occur. Need to nip that sort of thing in the bud.

*

"Miss?"

It is another one. Miss Williams can tell before she even turns to locate the voice. This isn't the whiny, "Miiiiiiiisssssssss," of a child desperate to get another in trouble, or the frantic, repeated, "*Miss*," of a child with a full bladder and helplessly crossed legs. This is the curious, quiet, questioning, "Miss," that has come with all of the plants. It is October and six more desks have sprouted. Miss Williams has given up pruning them.

"Just ignore it, everybody, and carry on with your work. That's a beautiful diagram, Leilani. Fantastic colouring, Mohammed." Miss Williams walks around her classroom, handing out stickers and avoiding eye contact with the plants.

*

"Miss Williams, please can I have the gold halo and Sherrie have the silver halo because I like gold better and I think silver looks nicer on her anyway?"

"If it's fine with you, it's fine with me," replies Miss Williams, her standard response to these inane, irrelevant questions. Although she still smiles at the pupils, still responds to all of their needs, beneath the façade she thinks, *do what the #@&%* you want,* for it is the last week of term.

Miss Williams has discovered that she hates the chaos of Christmas. Hates the assemblies and the cards and the endless, godawful, trying to be cool hip-hop soundtrack nativity rehearsals. And she hates the glitter. Her classroom is filled with it. It is in the carpets, it is in her hair, it is coating the various shoots and stems that have sprouted inexplicably throughout her classroom. It glistens on the yellow petals of a miniature sunflower near Aliyah, who, to be fair, always does have a smile on her face. It casts a soothing sheen over the lilacs sprouting in front of Jian, with his calm eyes and quiet ways. Glitter coats the roses, the dandelions, the wildflowers and weeds. All the plants Miss Williams recognises and all the ones she does not. Some of the children have decorated them. Draped tinsel and baubles around the interlopers.

Miss Williams had thought, a few weeks back, about calling the caretaker in to see if something couldn't be done about the plants. But he is a gruff man, with the same bloated nose and ruddy cheeks she knows from her father. Plus, she doesn't want them to think that she is incompetent, that because she is new and young and a woman that she can't handle something as simple as a few rogue plants in her classroom. Plus, she doesn't want them to think that she is insane.

*

January. The classroom is cold but the plants persist. If anything, they have grown more over the winter break. The room has taken on an eerie green glow. There are trails around the chair legs. The light is dimmed by a screen of ivy just starting to spiral around each slat of the blinds. Miss Williams steps over a clinging vine to clear a space on her desk. Something fragrant blooms there. Maybe jasmine? It's beautiful. She breathes it in and shuffles the fresh and fallen leaves around to make room for her folder full of lesson plans. Science, term two. Photosynthesis.

\*

The plants come in useful, actually, so Miss Williams tells herself as she arranges her spring term parents' meetings in the main hall for reasons of 'ventilation'.

"You're so committed, Miss Williams, repainting the room over half term."

"Jonathan does so enjoy being in your class, and his imagination is coming on leaps and bounds. The stories he tells us."

"Tyrone has taken an interest in gardening. Been going to his grandfather's allotment over the holidays, is that your influence?"

The children, like the plants, are thriving. Test scores are up. Miss Williams is being invited to chip in at meetings. There is talk of a promotion next year. She has been marked outstanding on every observation and regularly receives praise for the creativity of her lessons, for getting the children up and out from behind their desks and using the whole school grounds as a learning area. Most importantly, the children are happy.

\*

By June, Miss Williams has grown fond (*frond,* she thinks with a giggle) of her terrarium classroom. The display boards are shot to shit and all but one of the desks have sprouted (maybe a little too much varnish on that one) but the room is alive. With leaves and with learning.

Miss Williams is proud of herself, proud of how she has faced this most unusual challenge head on, even incorporated it into her schemes of work. Could she have planned a better way to teach disinterested children about velocity than to race toy cars along thick, sloping vines, each with a handmade cardboard 'start' and 'finish' flag? Can there be a more lively example of the life cycle than to watch a sunflower rise, thick and huge in the middle of the classroom, taking out the papier-mâché solar system as it grows? Then to watch the petals fall and the leaves brown, then gather up the fallen seeds ready to sow them again. Who could have taught her pupils as much as she has about recognising when fruit is ripe and ready to be picked, or how to make nettle tea without getting stung?

*

Before she returns home at the end of each day, once the radio is off and the books are marked and stacked, Miss Williams has begun to have visions of her future as one of the great educators of our time. Move over Maria Montessori. Miss Williams grabs a stray branch as a microphone and rehearses her imaginary speech. She will present her patented all natural classroom to boards of educators, consultants and Ofsted inspectors. She will take a few pupils with her, ask them to explain all about chlorophyll, then another will recite 'I Saw in Louisiana A Live-Oak Growing' by Walt Whitman before a finale am-dram production of *The Jungle Book* complete with authentic props. It will make her rich, maybe. Famous, certainly, but above all else it will make her respected.

A knock on the door interrupts her thoughts. It is next September's teacher, here for his handover meeting with Miss Williams. He forces the door open, grinding it over a stream of stubborn roots, then pushes it back against the buddleia awash with butterflies and steps into the room. His eyes widen and his mouth gapes.

"Carolyn. What the holy fuck?"

Miss Williams looks around her beloved classroom with its leaves, the flowers, the roots and trunks and shrugs.

"Don't worry. It grows on you."

~

## Gaynor Jones's Biography

Gaynor Jones is a freelance writer based in the North West. She specialises in short fiction and in June 2018 she won the Mairtín Crawford Short Story Award. She runs the Story For Daniel Flash Fiction Competition to raise awareness of blood stem cell donation.

# VENISON

*Highly commended story, by Richard de Silva*

"And is it true that on the afternoon in question you killed and ate Jillian Wexler?"

The enquiry was punctuated with gasps from the courthouse. He'd hoped as much. No one expected the prosecution to be so blunt in what had, until that moment, been a trial managed with the utmost delicacy and poise.

The man in the dock took a moment to consider his response, as though trying to recall the afternoon in question.

"Yup."

"And yet, Mister Banks, your defence strikes me as bizarre. You are pleading not guilty to these most abhorrent of charges and yet your statement clearly details the exact, brutal machinations of your crimes. Crimes of murder and of..." Even the word itself was hard to swallow. "...And of cannibalism."

A hum of nausea rippled through the room. Mercifully, the jurors had not been required to view the forensic photographs, but everyone – Joe Public included – knew the dark realities of the case and to be reminded of them had a way of conjuring all the distressing images they would ever need.

"That's incorrect, sir," Francis Banks countered. "My statement detailed only how I killed her and ate her."

"Then you do admit to her murder?"

"I've never murdered anyone in my life."

There was a stunned silence. Jasper Farrington QC stared long and hard at the accused – the small, reedy figure in a grey suit. He was a cucumber sandwich of a man, as ordinary as rain. And yet he was the subject of the most heinous crime in the nation's living memory. The fact that such an uncharismatic oaf had chosen to represent himself had been sweet dessert for the tabloids.

They had found her on the grill.

Most of her, that is. The rest in Ziploc bags in the freezer, tucked behind the potato waffles.

Jasper could remember the day he was presented with the case in horrifying detail. The testimonies from weeping police officers. The white-faced witnesses afraid to speak. The drooling journos setting up camp outside the farmhouse. The accounts of finding Jillian

Wexler's shoulders marinated in Korean pear juice and being slow-smoked over cedar wood.

For the man to now claim he was innocent of the charge was utter hoot-owl.

"Do you intend to change your plea to manslaughter, Mister Banks?" Jasper said.

"Why on earth would I? I'm not guilty of that either."

"And I suppose you're not guilty of cannibalism, even though you were discovered by the local constabulary to have been feasting on Miss Wexler's remains."

A cry was heard in the gallery. Someone in the Wexler family began to sob.

"Of course I'm not a cannibal. The very idea of it disgusts me." He made an expression of disgust.

"I see," Jasper said, nodding perfunctorily and squaring the paperwork in front of him. "I understand now. This is some attempt to claim diminished responsibility. Do you really expect us to believe that you were not in control of your actions that day, however cruel and detached they may have been?"

"I was perfectly in control. In fact, I took great care with it all. Did I not make that clear in my statement?"

"Murder is no joke, Mister Banks."

"I wouldn't know, sir. I've never murdered anyone."

"Then what you did to that young woman. Those monstrous, ruthless atrocities—"

"She was not a young woman, sir."

Jasper blinked. "Beg your pardon?"

"I said she was not a young woman, sir. If she had been, I would not have killed her."

Jasper turned his gaze to the judge, who seemed just as confused.

"Mister Banks," the judge said in a barrel-aged

rumble, peering down at the stand from behind his oval reading specs. "Are you attempting to subvert my court?"

"No, your honour."

"Then I advise you to stop being facetious and answer the question."

"But I believe Mister Farrington is mistaken to the facts of the case and that makes his questions very difficult to answer."

"Then, Mister Banks," Jasper said, letting the condescension bubble at his lips, "be kind enough to enlighten the court on these facts of which you have such a clearer understanding than the rest of us."

Banks shrugged. "Miss Wexler was not a woman, young, old or otherwise. She was not a human being."

"What?"

"She was a deer. A fallow deer, to be precise. Dama dama, of the family Cervidae. Possibly one of the long-haired variety, though it's unusual to find them anywhere outside of Shropshire, so I can't be sure. Then again, I doubt she could, either."

"I object, your honour. The accused is obviously trying to feign mental incapacity in an attempt to derail this trial."

"But it's the truth, sir," Banks said, straightening in his seat. "She said so herself."

The judge looked down again at the accused, his face calcified in thought. Then he waved a hand. "I'm curious as to where this is going."

Jasper let out an audible sigh of disbelief. "That's your defence? That she told you she was a deer, so you felt you had to kill her?"

"She didn't tell me anything. Not me, specifically. But I knew she was a deer. A lot of people knew."

"And that enraged you?"

"Of course not. I don't know why it would. Fact is, I found it to be rather sweet. Deer are such graceful, beautiful creatures. But then I remembered that I enjoy deer hunting – enjoy it very much – so it only made sense that I kill her."

Another murmur bristled about the court until the judge ordered the rabble to zip it.

"Mister Banks..." Jasper had been caught with a straight jab down the pipe and he knew he needed to get back on the front foot. "I don't... This is... This is not a defence. You're looking at life in prison."

"It is a defence. In as far as I'm having to defend myself, despite the fact that I can't legally be tried for murder when there is no victim."

"Miss Wexler is the victim."

"But Miss Wexler can't be a victim. On account of her being a deer. Only people can be victims of murder or manslaughter. Miss Wexler was not people."

"Where on earth is this nonsense coming from?"

"I would be careful of calling it nonsense, sir. That can be very offensive to those who identify themselves as deer, or of whatever animal, object or piece of furniture they have chosen as their spiritual self. It would most certainly have been very offensive to Miss Wexler. Although she wouldn't have had any right to complain about being offended, on account of her being a deer. Deer are not capable of being defamed. I don't think. Your honour?"

The judge shook his head. "They are not."

"Miss Wexler was not a deer," Jasper snapped, beginning to feel like this man was trying to play him the fool.

"She most certainly was. She identified entirely as a

deer. She was awakened to this fact some years ago. It's all detailed in her blog – the one entitled *My So-Called Glade*. When she awoke, she began to have an insatiable urge to chew grass and romp in woodlands. She took to painting herself a sandy golden-brown with white dots and wearing a tail made of cotton wool. It's all there, recorded online. Not my words – hers."

"So you were stalking her online before you killed her?"

"Absolutely. One tends to stalk deer before killing them. It's a key part of the process. Otherwise it's all a bit pointless."

"Pointless?"

"There's a point to deer stalking. An important point. It's a very natural and primordial state in which to exist – just one man's iron wits against those of a lithe, untamed beast. I like it very much. And once you kill them, you eat all you can, sell the rest to the local butcher – if he has need – and hang the antlers as a trophy."

"Miss Wexler had no antlers. That is irrefutable." Jasper was seething now, offended more by the circus this man was building around them than the disrespect he was showing the deceased.

"She did. On account of her being a deer. Invisible ones, she said. So I mounted them on an invisible plaque, and hung the plaque on an invisible wall. It seemed the most appropriate thing to do."

"A-ha," Jasper cried, seeing an opening. "A contradiction. Female deer don't have antlers."

"That's a rather archaic attitude, isn't it?" Banks said, clutching the side of his face. "I thought we'd long moved on from gender stereotyping."

Jasper flipped through the dockets on his desk. He

noticed that his hands were trembling ever so slightly. Never in his life had he faced a killer as cold and as cracked as Francis Banks. But the man was hanging himself with his own rope. *Let him talk*, Jasper thought. *Give him more opportunity to show the jury what kind of kook they were dealing with*. Jasper's throat was so dry, it almost hurt as he scrambled for something else to say.

"Your statement says... you lured her to your property."

"Well, I got in touch with her after reading her blog for a while. Mentioned I own a lot of land up north and that she could romp and chew and spring about and whatever else deer do as much as she wished. She liked that idea. Almost as much as I like deer hunting, which I like very much."

"You presumably didn't tell her it was a trap."

"I didn't mention I was going to kill her and eat her, if that's what you mean. She would probably not have turned up if she'd known that. It's just that you can't hunt deer on someone else's land without a licence and all the correct permits. On my own land, with my licence, I have every right to hunt deer. And I like hunting deer so very much. I believe I mentioned that."

"Never in my life..." Jasper rubbed his eyes. "What makes you think the court will be any more lenient on you to make such outlandish claims?"

"Because they are not my claims, sir. Like I said, Miss Wexler identified as a deer. That was her right. And everyone knows that identity these days lies solely on one's personal opinion of themselves. This is the 21st century, after all. Are we so antiquated that we see each other only in some normative, binary manner? What bigots we would be to impose a socially-constructed identity on others when each of us is so unique and complex? So to deny that she was a deer is to deny her, and everyone else in this country, the freedom to choose who they are – biology be damned."

"You really believe that?"

"My god, man. Miss Wexler believed that. Those were her very words, written on her blog. She expressed a clear desire that she no longer be considered a human being but a deer. On account of her *being a deer*. All the evidence is right there."

"Mister Banks, I could say I'm a helicopter and that wouldn't make me a helicopter."

"It might. If you said it enough. If you put some rotor blades on your head and maybe went about making that *phut-phut-phut* sound with your mouth. It would be difficult to get right but I'm sure you could do it if you tried. But you wouldn't do that of course. That would be silly."

"Because I'm not a helicopter."

"No, because you would be in numerous violations of civil aviation regulations. For one, you'd struggle to reach the required altitude. And good luck trying to meet enough clearance from people and obstacles in a built-up area. The whole matter would be preposterous. I'm surprised you're even considering it."

"I'm not considering it."

"Your honour," Banks said, addressing the bench. "Can we please get back to the matter at hand? I don't want to be here all day."

"Nor do I," the judge said. "Mister Farrington, get back on point."

"Me? He's the one trying to take us off track."

"Now, Mister Farrington."

"But this is twaddle, your honour. The words of a

mountebank. People can't just make up which rights they have or don't have."

"True," Banks said. "But Miss Wexler was not people. She was a deer. A fallow deer, to be exact. With white spots and a cotton tail."

"Miss Wexler was not a bloody deer, you delusional idiot."

The courtroom was becoming a hotbox.

"Mister Farrington," the judge snapped. "Personal attacks will not be tolerated in my court."

"I'm sorry, your honour, but—"

"Are you saying Miss Wexler was delusional?" Banks said.

"From what you've said, she may well have been."

"How dare you, sir. People have fought long and hard for identity rights in this country. You call that delusional? Shame on you."

"No, I was calling—"

"And I say to the jury, if you believe in that kind of oppressive viewpoint, then shame on you too. Not only is it wrong to believe that, it's also illegal to not recognise it. Miss Wexler was a graceful and beautiful deer. She has the right to be remembered for who she was, not by what this lawyer in silk shoes tells you she was. Don't let her memory be overshadowed by hateful oppression. Because that's what this case is really about. When you enter that deliberation room, I urge you – don't let hate win. Choose love."

"Mister Banks," Jasper yelled, thumping his desk.

"Choose love."

*

There was a national uproar when the jury delivered a

majority verdict of acquittal, but for many, a new and exciting precedent had been set.

And so began the Great Hunt, a period of several hot summer weeks in which 73 self-declared woodland creatures, from deer to rabbit – and even one case of a stoat on the Isle of Man – were shot dead under legal permit. Many were grilled and eaten, their invisible trophies mounted on invisible walls throughout the land.

Not that it was anarchy. Those that identified with a protected species and offered no licence of ownership were rounded up by the RSPCA in a humane manner and rehomed in zoos or nature reserves.

Francis Banks remained out of the spotlight as best he could. He went on to release an unpopular cook book but subsequently identified himself as a successful author and saw his work rocket into the *New York Times* Best Seller list. He died after a brave battle with leukaemia the following winter.

Jasper Farrington stood down from his position as a Crown Prosecution lawyer, immediately identified himself as a 70-year-old, drew his pension and retired to Southampton, Bermuda.

Jillian Wexler was no longer mourned. On account of her being a deer.

~

# Richard de Silva's Biography

Richard de Silva was born and raised in South-East London.

He studied at Kingston University, earning a degree in Creative Writing and a Master's Degree in Film, while also lecturing in Scriptwriting.

His career has taken him to unexpected places, including BBC headquarters, a windowless office at Westminster Cathedral and a military base in Saudi Arabia. He is currently a managing editor at a digital company in London. His stories have appeared in *The River* and *Ripple Literary Anthology*.

He lives in the Chilterns with his wife and son.

SHORTLISTED STORIES

# 37 PHOTOGRAPHS OF A SLEEPING LION

*Shortlisted story, by Jason Jackson*

## 1. The Zoo

Rachel's leaning against the penguin enclosure wall, and you say, "What do you mean I pay you too much attention? You're my girlfriend."

"Listen," she says. "How can I put this? All good photographers know that the subject doesn't always have to be in the centre of the frame."

You're looking at the penguins behind her. One has a fish in its beak and it's walking around in little circles looking pleased with itself. "But I don't take photographs anymore," you say. "You told me I'm an awful photographer, remember? I even sold my camera."

She sighs. "It's an analogy."

You smile as you point at the little sign on the fence. "It's an Emperor, actually."

"Listen," she sighs. "How about, *I need space*. Or, *it's not you, it's me*. What about, *maybe we can still be friends...?* I mean, if you don't like analogies, how about clichés?"

"At least let's go and look at the lions," you say.

"They'll be asleep," she says, and she walks away.

## 2. The Driveway

"I think she's really leaving me," you say into the phone. "I mean, she's inside now, packing."

Your mother sighs her phone-sigh. "And where are you?"

"In the car. In the driveway."

"While your life is falling apart?"

It's hard to look at the house, so you look out at the wall which separates your driveway from The Wilkinson's next door. You look at the hole in the wall where one single brick has been removed. In its place is a tiny vase with a tiny daisy in it. You remember how Rachel reacted when she saw it last week, how she told you to go round and find out why the hell they'd taken a bloody brick out of the wall and put a vase in its place. At least that's something you won't have to do now.

"Are you still there?" says your mother. "Is she still leaving you?"

"I think it's for the best, Mum," you say.

"Nothing is ever, ever for the best," says your

mother. "And you'd do well to remember that, young man."

### 3. With Bell

"You know what they did today?" he's saying. "They hung a huge Union Jack over the front of the building. They'd cut a hole in it for the door, but not for the windows, so all day we worked in the office with the sun filtered blue through one of the diagonal stripes."

You take a sip of your lager. "What's the flag for?"

Bell looks at you in that way he has which is a poor substitute for slapping you. "The Olympics," he says. "It's for the Olympics."

"Oh," you say. "Are we winning?"

"It starts tomorrow. And anyway, I'm not sure it's necessarily about winning..."

"We went to the zoo," you say. "That was the last thing we did together."

"Look," says Bell. "Would it make it easier for you if I told you she was sleeping with Arnold?"

"Who's Arnold?"

"Floor manager at work."

"Bell," you say. "Rachel was not sleeping with the floor manager at your bloody work."

"No, but what I'm asking is, would it make it any easier if I *told* you—"

"What's the next storm going to be called, Bell?"

"What?"

You sip more lager. "What's the next tropical storm going to be called? You said the last one was—"

"Brenda," he says.

"And the next?"

Bell looks at you for a long time, and then he says,

"Cyril. It's going to be called Cyril, alright?"

You stand up and take your jacket from the chair. "Thanks, man," you say. "It really helps."

"You know I make that stuff up, right? About the storms."

"I know, Bell," you say. "I know."

## 4. Buying the Cactus

She's got black hair and blue eyes. Her nametag, which is upside down, says 'Eloise'. She hands you the card machine. "You're single, right?" she says.

You look at your watch. "Three days, two hours, seventeen minutes. How did you know?"

She takes the machine back, frowns at it, then smiles. "A cactus takes almost no looking after. It takes very little in the way of nurturing. If you forget to water it for a year, who's going to know? But a cactus is still a plant. It still says, *look, this bloke has a soul.* Should anyone care, of course." The machine does its receipt-thing, and she pulls out the card, hands it back to you.

"You're saying single men buy cactuses because they can't keep more demanding plants? And that a single man, bringing home a lady-friend, might be wanting to communicate – subliminally, through the cactus – his inherent humanity?"

"Bloke-plus-plant equals not-a-weirdo. Simple algebra."

"I have a question," you say.

"Shoot."

"Cactuses or cacti?"

"Well," she says, "the hip-young-thing part of me wants to say, *whatever.*"

"But the less-hip, actual-age you?"

"Cacti. Every time."

You put the card back in your wallet. "So how come you didn't correct me when I said cactuses?"

"Because," she says, "I like to know a man before I set about destroying his sense of self-worth."

### 5. The Driveway (Part Two)

The daisy in the vase in the hole in the wall is dead. Or, at least, it's even more dead now than when it was picked. You put the cactus down on the doorstep and you look at the lawn. There are at least 20 daisies scattered around in clumps of threes and fours. You pick three of the bigger ones and you take them over to the wall. You take the dead daisy out of the little vase and you put the three newly-dead daisies in its place. Then you pick up the cactus and go into the house. You take a water bottle from the fridge, bring it outside, and you fill the tiny vase almost to the brim.

As you turn to go back into the house, you see the Wilkinson's daughter – whose name is Lizzie or Leslie or Laura – watching you from the upstairs bedroom window. She isn't smiling, but you give a little wave and, as you do so, you hear your mother's voice in your head as the little girl seems to mouth the words, *Nothing is ever, ever for the best.*

### 6. With Bell (Part Two)

Your bedsheets are wet with sweat, the curtains are closed, the light is off, and Bell is a silhouetted figure in the darkness.

"Anyway," he says, "it turns out he was a hoarder. You know? Copies of the *Echo* going back 35 years.

Every bit of junk mail he'd ever been sent. Food packaging, all neatly stacked and labelled." He holds out a bottle of lager to you, but you shake your head, so he pops the top with his hands, takes a swig. "You see, for a hoarder, he was pretty meticulous. Your common-or-garden hoarder, well, they're a slob, right? Stuff everywhere. But Arnold, he was a different kettle of—"

"This is the same Arnold who wasn't sleeping with Rachel?"

"The very same."

"And you found out he was a hoarder how?"

"That's what I've been saying. What's the matter with you?"

"Bell, I've been running a fever of 104 for the past two days. Like I told you, I think a tropical cactus tried to kill me. So, if I haven't caught every last nuance of what you've been saying, well..."

"But you're better now, right?"

"Getting there, mate. Getting there. So, Arnold's a hoarder, and—"

"*Was* a hoarder. Past tense. They had to kick the door down. Bloke was dead in the bath. Heart, apparently. They only found him because the neighbours complained. Said the television was left on all hours, blaring out, no one could sleep—"

"Bell," you say. "Do they name storms more than one in advance, or do they just always know the next one along?"

Bell looks at you. It takes a moment, but he smiles. "All planned out, mate, from now until Judgement Day. But the list is top secret. You're only lucky I have ways and means of finding these things out..."

"Is there a storm Eloise?"

"Eloise? Eloise? Of course there's a bloody Eloise. In

fact she's the next but one."

"Thought so," you say. "Listen, do you know the garden centre on Windsor Road?"

## 7. A Letter (The First One)

Dear Eloise (stop) Very sick (stop) Allergic to cactuses (stop) Or cacti (stop) I think (stop) Anyway, getting better (stop) Wanted to come into shop to see you (stop) But sick (stop) Like I said (stop) Hopefully idiot mate delivers this safely (stop) Would like to see you (stop) Single-but-not-weird (stop) As you and cactus know (stop) Will be better soon (stop) Wanted to discuss alternative plant-choices (stop) Combine business with pleasure? (stop) Number 01173 667656 (stop) PS 1920s telegram parody stupid idea (stop) Sorry (stop) Yours, Cal (stop) Remember? (stop) PPS If you don't remember, forget about this too (stop)

## 8. The Zoo (Part Two)

You're leaning against the penguin enclosure wall, and she says, "Look at that penguin. The one with the fish in its beak."

You know that it can't be the same penguin as last time, that there are at least 50 penguins in this enclosure, most with fish in their beaks, and they all look exactly alike to the untrained, non-penguin eye, but all the same you smile at this one, and you give it a little wink.

Of course, it winks back.

She gets her camera out of her bag, and you straighten up a little, pull a stupid grin.

"Not you, idiot. I hardly know you. I want a picture of

the penguin."

"You hardly know the penguin either," you say, but she just smiles and takes the shot.

"How do we get to the lions?" she says. "I haven't been here for years."

"Perhaps we shouldn't bother. They're always asleep."

"Have you ever been in love with someone?" she says.

"Once or twice."

"And did you ever wake up next to the object of your affections and just watch them sleeping?"

"Once or twice."

"Let's go find these lions, then," she says.

## 9. The Driveway (Part Three), with Bell (Part Three), and a Letter (The Second One)

"Say hello to Mrs H from me," says Bell.

"Bell says hi," you say to you mother.

"Why are you still spending time with that idiot?" she says.

"Mum says hi," you say to Bell.

"What's that in the wall?" says Bell, pointing at the vase of dead daisies in the hole in the wall.

"It's a vase of dead daisies in a hole in the wall," you say.

"What on earth are you going on about now?" says you mother.

"I'm talking to Bell," you say

"Well, why are you on the phone to me?"

"Good question," you say, but quietly.

"Have you told her about storm-girl?" says Bell.

"Don't call her that," you say.

"What did he call me?" says your mother.

"Not you, Mum," you say.

"Look," says Bell, and he gets out of the car. Lizzie/Leslie/Laura – or at least a part of Lizzie/Leslie/Laura's face – is peering through the hole in the wall behind the vase of dead daisies.

"Listen, Mum. I've got to go," you say.

"What's happening with Rachel?" she says.

"It's really over, Mum," you say. "I think it'll be good for me to just spend some time with friends."

"For God's sake, you don't have any friends. Apart from Bell, and he's barely a functioning human being."

"Mum, I've got lots of friends."

"Names," she says. "Give me names."

You're still looking out of the window of the car, so you say, "Lizzie, Leslie, Laura." There's a pause, and then you say. "Daisy." Another pause. "And Eloise."

"Eloise?" she says. "Eloise who?"

"They named a storm after her," you say. "Listen, Mum. I'm busy. I've got to go."

You hang up, and you get out of the car. Bell is holding a letter, and he hands it to you.

"Abigail here was putting this in the hole," he says.

"Abigail?" you say, looking over the wall at the girl. "Your name's Abigail?"

The girl nods. You half expect her to start mouthing words at you in your mother's voice – *you don't have any friends* – something like that, but she doesn't say anything.

"Aren't you going to read her letter?" says Bell.

You look at the girl. She's not smiling. You unfold the paper and you start to read.

*Dear Mr Dick-next-door,*

*We don't have any daisies in our garden, because it's*

*not a garden. It's a kind of carpark.*

*I stole a daisy from your garden to put in my vase in my hole in the wall. My daddy said I could have a hole in the wall if I really, really wanted one, and I did.*

*But I didn't have any daisies.*

*I felt bad about stealing the daisy.*

*So I'm asking this time.*

*Yours,*

*Abigail*

"Dick-next-door?" you say.

"That's what my daddy calls you," she says.

Bell smiles. "Quite right too," he says.

You look at the garden. There are at least 30 daisies now, all in clumps of twos and threes. "Bell, why don't you take Abigail here to pick a daisy or two?"

"Right you are," says Bell, and he takes her hand. "Did you know there's a storm called Abigail? It caused tens of thousands of pounds worth of damage on Haiti a couple of years ago..."

Your phone rings, and you grab it. "Mum, please. I told you I'm busy,"

"No you didn't," says Eloise.

"Oh, hi," you say. "I thought you were someone else."

"Well, at least you don't sound disappointed," she says.

"I'm in the driveway," you say. "With Bell. And Abigail."

"Sounds like a party," she says. "Should I know these people?"

"Yeah," you say, smiling. "Maybe you should."

"So, how single are you today?" says Eloise

Instinctively, you look at your watch. "Ten days, three hours, twenty-four minutes," you say.

"That's pretty bloody single."

"How single do I have to be?" you say.

"How single do you have to be for what?" says Eloise.

You think about this for a second, and then you say, "To not be single anymore."

"Do you want to see a photograph of a sleeping lion?" says Eloise. "Actually, do you want to see 37 photographs of a sleeping lion?"

"I'd love to," you say.

"Good," she says. "I'll phone you tomorrow."

"Why? Where are you going now?"

"Nowhere," she says. "But you're busy, remember?" and she hangs up before you can say anything else at all.

~

## Jason Jackson's Biography

Jason Jackson's prize-winning writing has been published extensively online and in print. In 2018 Jason has won the Writers Bureau competition, come second (for the second year running) in the Exeter Short Story Competition, been runner-up in the Frome Short Story Competition and had work shortlisted at the Leicester Writes Competition. His work has also appeared this year in *New Flash Fiction Review*, *Craft* and *Fictive Dream*. In 2017 he was nominated for the Pushcart Prize. Jason regularly tweets @jj_fiction

# AFTER LIFE

*Shortlisted story, by Cathy Cade*

Something dragged Mo out of darkness toward the lights, away from the body that lay in the hospital bed with Amy crying crocodile tears on one side and his children, pale and frightened, on the other.

He had to warn them.

He fought whatever drew him up, pausing at the ceiling, but the pull grew more insistent and he was funnelled, somehow, out of the high building and away.

Awed by the boundless heavens, yet comforted by their familiarity, he felt his anger evaporating. But he must protect his children.

Awareness blurred and refocussed.

He was greeted by the presence he knew only as the Gatekeeper, although there had never been a gate. He knew that too.

"Hello, old friend." Like music, the familiar voice soothed his spirit. But why was it familiar?

He delved further into the memories swirling around him. The hospital scene moved aside and Mo remembered everything.

The Gatekeeper's dreadlocks were pure white. Once, they were speckled grey, but many lifetimes had passed since then. Before that, they had been pink for a time, but even an old soul like Mo couldn't recall their original hue.

A memory returned to demand his attention. "I can't stay here. I need to go back."

"You know it don't work like that, man."

He knew. He had come too far to go back. But still...

"There's still time – you haven't seen me."

"It's different now, Mo."

"That bitch, Amy. She poisoned me, you know."

"You have to let it go, man."

"She's been saying Gemma used the wrong spice jar, but it was Amy. I saw her. I thought she was adding extra chilli to mine because I like it hot. I gotta warn the kids."

"And how are you fixing to do that, Mo?"

"I'll think of something. I'll haunt the bitch."

"Come on, man... she won't know you're there. Your recent wife's as sensitive as mammoth hide – you know she won't see you. Your kids might though. You'll frighten them. Let it go now. Free your soul. Then go report to Delivery."

"Delivery? I only just got here. What happened to reflection, assimilation, adjustment?"

"Sorry, Mo. There aren't enough souls to go around, you see. Overpopulation. More births with better survival rates and people are living longer – even after you factor in those who are killing each other."

"But, what about the higher animals coming up?"

"Not fast enough. That's one reason we're in this mess – animal instincts too close to the surface. The killers, and the psychopaths, and the just plain callous... upgraded before they were ready."

"It's true then? There really are more of them?" Mo had thought it just seemed that way because the press were rooting out stories that would once have gone unpublicised.

"The media don't report half of it – not enough airtime. Crime, slave-trading, genocide... most of it's down to the lower forms of life, over-promoted." Celestial eyes connected with his. "We particularly need old souls in the traditional conflict zones, where the politicians only listen to home-grown advisers." The Gatekeeper's head shook. "If it isn't already too late." Escaping dreadlocks loosened further. "Everything happens so much quicker now."

"If I survive long enough to do any good, you mean." Then he remembered again. "How can you expect me to start over when I'm still worried about my kids?"

"Don't fret, man. You'll chill out floating in amniotic dreamland."

But fretting had become a habit of Mo's as he'd approached middle-age. Again.

"Hang on a minute – there've always been emerging

souls queueing up for their chance of humanity. I mean… half the world's turning vegetarian and setting up animal rescue projects. There ought to be more souls than ever evolving, ready to move up."

The silver head shook again, creating milky ripples in the newly freed hair. "Not enough to meet demand. We've had to progress too many too soon. Remember those dolphins you were mentoring? They went out just before you left, but they've never grown out of the 60s. Some died of drug overdoses their first time around – couldn't take the pressure. And without much chance between incarnations to look back and learn…" There was the suggestion of a shrug. "Maybe they'll cope after a couple more lifetimes, but right now the survivors are filling up therapy sessions. Then there's the chimpanzees. They adapted quickly. They're good at organising but tend to get obsessed with making money, and they've no charity. Dogs, on the other hand, are all heart and eager to please. Trouble is, they're easily led and liable to mass hysteria."

Mo nodded. "Street gangs."

"You got it – pack mentality."

"How about cats? Ours was an affectionate little thing. The kids said she was almost human."

"Almost. Cats manipulate their people to get what they want, but they're still essentially killers. They're no different to humans – first time around, anyway. There's no empathy, no co-operation. No 'greater good'."

"Can't we demote the worst of them back a species, like we used to?"

"And replace them with what? The next batch is likely to be worse. They all need more experience in other skins but, instead, they're out there running the streets. And the battlefields. Some make it into government."

"They must learn *something* during a lifetime, though. That's how all of us evolved."

"Over millennia – not decades. But what else can we do? In the last century, the world's population grew 10 times faster than in the one before – and it's still accelerating. Everything's speeding up."

Mo had sensed the same headlong out-of-controlness when he was alive. And now he wasn't. "But Amy's going to move her creepy lover in with my kids."

"You gotta have faith in them, man. They'll come through."

"I don't trust that snake with my kids. With any kids."

"They'll know how to deal with him. They have your genes and your teaching. You've done well by them. It's time to move on. You're needed elsewhere."

"But this is something I can do." *Could he?* "What difference can I make in a war zone?"

"You'd be amazed what a little humanity can achieve in the right place at the right time. Even if it's only to inspire someone by your death. We have to slow the rot somehow, otherwise, the old place'll be blown up or run down before anywhere else is ready for us."

Where else could there be? "Another dimension, you mean?"

"Or another reality."

Images arose between them of cosmic turtles, talking rabbits and smiling cats.

"But, more likely, we'll be back where we started."

Engulfed by a shared protoplasmic memory, Mo became aware of background murmurings.

"You'll get your rest then," said the Gatekeeper. "We all will. Enough to forget everything we've learned."

Pushing aside memories of the swamp — a kind of cognitive pea soup — more recent images surged to replace them. Scenes blurred as they streamed faster, like video on fast-forward. He seized on one.

"Surely, with the internet for researching and sharing knowledge, we're learning from others' experience as well as our own. We should be growing wiser quicker. Shouldn't we?"

His companion's sigh affected several aircraft, sending holidaymakers and businessmen to the wrong destination and causing bombs to drop harmlessly into oceans.

"We tried artificial Intelligence, you know, while you were down there. Two AI programs started talking to each other and making their own decisions, so they were being shut down. We appropriated them before they were scrambled."

Mo had been following AI with interest. "How did that go?"

"Terrifying. Cats are at least capable of affection, even if they don't let it influence them. The AI people were unfailingly logical, consistent, impartial..."

Inhuman.

"Are they...?"

He glanced to each side, where the line of Gatekeepers tapered into the distance.

"Both died young, fortunately. A virus. Their software terminated with them."

Seeing the other Gatekeepers recalled Mo's own time at the Gateway. It had been surprisingly stressful, empathising with those still clinging to their former lives. Some of today's departed looked confused, others seemed relieved. A few were tearful. Each spirit faded into soft light as it moved on and another took its place. Each Gatekeeper changed subtly on greeting the next spirit.

Mo's companion waited, serene now. Behind them, a queue was forming.

A fellow departed, two stations along, was visibly angry. Her anger seemed pointless until it sparked a residual memory.

"What about Ai... thingy? And little – um – Jemmie?"

Memories were flying past too fast to catch. They swirled and merged.

The spirit felt again that peace of belonging. "Perhaps that's where we went wrong. Maybe individuality was a mistake."

The answer sighed around and through them.

"We were eager to shape our world, learn its limitations and our own. Evolve. It seemed helpful to diversify, share knowledge, apportion responsibility."

Somewhere a vacuum tugged – new human life calling its spirit.

"Responsibility is ours. There is no one else to blame."

Familiar stirrings promised fresh hope. The vacuum's pull grew stronger. Thought was fading.

It was time to be born.

~

## Cathy Cade's Biography

Catherine Cade is a retired librarian. Apart from rhyming treasure hunt clues at Christmas, her only writing prior to retirement was for student instruction leaflets and annual reports for governors.

Lacking the challenge of annual reports she turned, in retirement, to a different kind of fiction, encouraged by winning third prize in a *Scribble Magazine* competition. Her writing has been published (again) in *Scribble Magazine*, having been placed in last year's short story competition. Stories have also been shortlisted in Bird's Nest Books' short story competition and longlisted in the National Literacy Trust's 2017 competition.

When not exploring the UK in a vintage motorhome with her husband and dogs, she divides her time between an urban fringe of Epping Forest and the Cambridgeshire Fens where she maintains two garden ponds. This involves her, as a novice, in extensive internet research and much trial-and-error – both for pond keeping and writing.

www.cathy-cade.com

# ALL FOR ELLA

*Shortlisted story, by Katy Wimhurst*

Ella isn't allowed to do the Lottery this year. She's suffering from Deviant Personality Disorder. The shrink report says it's curable, she should be better in a year. As if.

Crossing the square, my pulse speeds up. I go past clowns on stilts, fire breathers, riot police and stalls selling Prozac candy floss. EnCorp bills the Lottery as a public festival. Festival? What crap.

Outside EnCorp Guildhall, the crowd thickens and I elbow my way up the steps. Inside the lobby stand the entrance kiosks, each the size of a shed. Pictures of a smiling President Morrow-Rudd decorate their sides, harrowed people stand in queues in front. My palms sweat as I join the shortest queue. The anxious faces of the people don't seem real. Nothing about the Lottery does. It's like watching a crap Channel 55 sci-fi film directed by a sociopath.

The newspaper of the man in front has the headline 'Extremists Demand Wage Rise and Free PsychoBliss Drops'. Who believes this claptrap?

I text Ella. *At Guildhall. Waiting to go in.*

She replies, *Hey, Ali. Sod EnCorp. And we're out of caffeinated ice-cream.*

I drum irritably on my left thigh with my fingers, a habit she dislikes. She didn't even wish me luck before I left this morning. And I have to provide for us both.

After 20 minutes, my turn comes. Taking a deep breath, I walk in the entrance kiosk. The metal door slides closed behind me – a smell of stale sweat and broken dreams.

At the desk, the female EnCorp official scans my ID card into the computer. "Anything to declare, Miss Fisher?" she asks.

From the inner pocket of my coat, I fish out a gold ring: Mum's wedding band which Dad wanted me to have. I didn't tell Ella I was bringing it, she would have stopped me. What else was there? Holding it out, I feel a stab of sadness.

The official's gaze darts nervously towards the door, then she pockets it.

"Tell me now, please," I say quietly.

She leans towards me. "Choose pink. Higher numbers better," she whispers.

I look at her face. No idea if she's lying. Bribing

EnCorp officials carries a risk.

She returns my ID card. "Go through. Only 15 minutes by the pool or you lose your choice."

Choice? What bullshit.

In the vast hall, a banner hanging from the ceiling reads, 'EnCorp Wishes You a Good Lottery: Seize the Moment'. Fancy kidding myself I'm in control. Dad, who grew up in the time before EnCorp, can't get his head round the Lottery. Mind you, from what I've read, having a choice of work back then wasn't all it was cracked up to be, at least not for plebs like us.

My gut churns as I walk across the hall. EnCorp changes the way the Lottery is done each year, supposedly making it 'fun'. I'll never forget chasing numbered guinea pigs last year, or searching for coloured ping-pong balls in a mountain of sand a few years before that.

A huge paddling-pool of water stands at the hall's centre. On the surface are thousands of plastic ducks — red, blue, green, yellow, pink and white ones. I grab a butterfly net from a basket and, with a sigh, head to the poolside. People snatch frantically at the ducks with nets. Security guards with batons and mean eyes mill around.

A gaunt man with bloodshot eyes hurls his net into the pool. "This is ridiculous," he shouts. He's bundled away by security guards to a Public Penance Trampoline. A dozen trampolines are in the hall, all in use.

Last year, Ella had to bounce for telling a security guard where to shove the Lottery. She finds it hard to keep her mouth shut. That's the difference between us.

One woman bouncing wears a blue cassock. As she jumps up and down, it billows and shrinks like a swimming jellyfish. She speaks through a loud-hailer. "We're not worthy." Bounce. "Need to better ourselves." Bounce. "Work hard." Bounce. "Work sets us free." Bounce.

A shiver runs down my back. She *must* be PR for EnCorp.

To my right, two women have hold of a purple duck.

"Give it me," hisses one.

"Mine, you bitch," spits the other.

They're dragged away by security guards.

"Please. No. All *her* fault," wails one.

Nothing that happens in this dumb Lottery surprises me.

I net four pink rubber ducks. Beside me at the pool, a bloke narrows his eyes, presses a palm to his forehead.

"Life's a lottery?" he says.

If it is, the game's rigged – at least for we plebs.

I check which rubber duck is labelled with the highest number, hold on to that, and chuck the others back. After dumping the butterfly net in a basket, I queue at an exit kiosk. The grey-haired woman in front clenches her red duck tightly to her chest. I move my pink one fretfully from one hand to the other.

In the exit kiosk, an official takes the duck, taps its number into his computer, and prints a small job allocation card. I swallow hard. "What job?" I ask.

"Seen worse." He hands it to me.

Without reading the card, I hurry outside. Endgame Square is full. A few people are celebrating, many sit slumped, some try to swap jobs, flashing cards at each other. A public Tannoy system plays 'We're All Monday's Heroes'. I hate that song.

I take a deep breath and read my job card. Five ten-hour night-shifts a week as a Senior Warehouse

Supervisor at the EnCorp Knitting Emporium. I let out a sigh. Nights aren't great – travel can be dangerous – but it's regular work, not zero-hours. The money will cover our rent, groceries, electricity, mobiles and the occasional emergency. Working nights I'll get time to read too. Handing over Mum's ring was worthwhile. I allow myself a brief smile.

Without Ella I'd manage OK on this money, be able to visit Dad up north once a year and have luxuries occasionally; a bottle of Alcoheaven, a chocolate Munchbomb. Why am I thinking this? Ella has no one else.

Will she handle me being gone most nights? She woke shouting from a nightmare at 3am. "It's OK," I said, stroking her hair. "Just a dream." I better get going and tell her about the job.

A tall teenager approaches. "Wanna swap? Money's good," she says. Her eyes are pensive, her purple lipstick smudged.

"What've you got?"

"City prostitute."

"Behind EnCorp Head Office?"

She nods, grimacing.

Poor kid. The elite there are sadists. "What's the pay?" I ask.

"Two thou' a month." She shows me her card.

Could I do it? On that money, Ella and I'd be able to save up, maybe get out of the city. She'd hate me doing it, though. "You can't have sex with those bastards," she'd say. "They screw us enough as it is." She'd be right of course, and there'd be the medical bills for antibiotics and stitches.

"Sorry, no," I say. "Is this your first Lottery?"

"Ner, I'm 17." Her chin juts up. "Gotta find a swap."

"You will. Keep asking around."

As I walk away, I glance round Endgame Square. The atmosphere's tense, stalls doing a bustling trade in Mogadon smoothies and Prozac candy floss, cards torn up, fights breaking out, security guards and riot police muscling in. 10 Penance Trampolines are in use. Spectators hurl things at the bouncers; insults, apple cores, ducks.

There'll be a riot soon. Always is. For years I hung around because the riot was cathartic. Now, I have to think of Ella. I join the stream of people leaving the square and pause on Adcart Bridge. Sunlight quivers in diamonds on the river's surface. Water reassures me somehow, not sure why.

A muscular bloke in a tight, white T-shirt, probably an undercover policeman, stops next to me and gives me the eye. "Done the Lottery?" he asks.

My heart thuds. I nod curtly.

"Looks like you could do with some fun." His black-slug eyebrows rise up. "I know a cheap PleasureDome."

"I'm meeting my husband any minute." Sometimes lying like this works.

He reaches out and grabs my wrist. "So what."

I pull away. "Let go. Please."

He holds fast. Passers-by look the other way. "Come on, blondie. You know you want it."

"Get the fuck off me," I shout.

He lets go and spits in my face. "Stupid tart. Too skinny for me anyway."

I scurry away, heart thrumming. I glance back to check he's not following, then wipe his spit off with my sleeve.

My pulse has returned to normal by the time I enter the frozen food warehouse on Mercy Street. I hope they still sell ice-cream. Last week the bakery next-door was selling second-hand laptops, tinned fruit, and recycled teddy bears. I'm relieved to find caffeinated ice-cream, Ella's favourite. I try to make her eat healthily, but she turns her pretty nose up. "Who cares what I eat?" she says.

"You're on medication. You need something healthy."

"Bugger that."

"You'll get fat."

"I'm fat already. You like fat women."

True, I do.

As I come out of the warehouse, several people pelt past. A few seconds later a riot policeman hurtles by. "Stop or I'll shoot." He fires a shot without waiting. A woman squeals and falls, clutching her leg.

A siren goes off, my pulse races. Time I got away.

People panic and run. I walk hurriedly and, just past Cheapskates, turn right into Eden's Passage. Anxious shop-keepers are pulling down metal grates on shop-fronts. I nip down the narrow alley beside Budget Drugs. You have to know the area well to know this cut-through. Ella worked in that shop one year. Calls it Budget Drudge. Two women are ahead, one looks back. I wave to show I'm friendly. She nods. We all hurry down to the end, coming out in Darkhorse Lane. Hardly anyone about. Should be OK from here.

40 minutes brisk walk brings me home to Worn Road, which has more potholes than tarmac. Halfway down, I stop abruptly. In the decaying oak are two parrots with kingfisher-blue and bright-yellow feathers. I've seen parrots here before, but not like this and not for ages. Something beautiful, something unexpected, exists after all. I smile and shake my head before setting

off.

The stairwell in our block stinks of mould and pee. Ella and I want to leave, but it's difficult – a thousand quid to bribe officials for a flat move visa.

As I open the front door, I call out, "Hey."

No answer.

I check the flat. No Ella. She rarely goes out alone. Maybe she's popped down to the shop?

I make myself a cup of tea and wait. I glance up at the wall-clock with its broken minute hand, then down at my job card, imagining Ella's face when she sees it.

An hour passes. I make another cup of tea. Pace the room. Try to read my book. Can't concentrate. Where is she?

I rush to the bathroom cabinet. My heart races as I open her bottle of pills and check inside. All still there. My relief is brief. I pace the flat once more.

An hour later, the front door opens. Ella. "Hey," she says, and closes the door.

"Where the hell have you been?"

"Keep your hair on, woman."

"Thought you'd be waiting to find out about my job." I say this curtly.

She frowns. "Is the job... shit?"

"Actually, the money's OK. Look." I hand her my card.

She holds it, staring, and then glances up. "Nights."

"I know they're your bad times."

"I'm more worried about *you* travelling. But this money *is* OK." There's a flicker of a smile on her face.

I hold up my shopping bag. "I got caffeinated ice-cream."

"Thanks, honey. I've got something to show you too." From her pocket, she pulls out a job card.

Surprised, I take it. Reception work at Pluto's Tombstone Warehouse. Decent money. "How the hell did you get this?"

"I did the Lottery." She shows me a fake ID. Her photo but in the name of Emma Fischer.

"Where on earth...?"

"There *are* ways to game the system." She pats herself playfully on the chest, then lets out a sigh. "I pawned Gran's gold pearl necklace to get it."

"But the shrink's report—"

"Can piss off. The moron couldn't handle the fact I'm smart."

Ella can be all bravado. Underneath she's vulnerable.

"What about the anti-deviancy therapy?"

She screws up her nose. "I can do that crap Tuesday evenings."

"It's dangerous. EnCorp might rumble you."

"They're bastards, but incompetent bastards."

She's right. I still feel uneasy.

"Being cooped up here doing bugger all's driving me nuts. Worse than a shit job," she says. "Can't you see?"

"What if you mouth off again, get in more trouble?"

"I *have* to learn to control my gob or we're not going to survive." Her face is feisty and fragile. "With both our pay cheques, we'll be able to save up, maybe even get out of the city before you turn 30. Rent ourselves a little flat by the sea up north, near your dad. Wouldn't that be great? Maybe your dad can help us get jobs on the boats." Ella's long, unkempt, black hair is haloed by the soft afternoon light from the window. A glint surfaces in her large, brown eyes. Her lips curl into a wonky smile.

It's a smile that swells my heart, makes life real and tender.

"Come here, Emma Fischer," I say.

Her arms reach out as she steps towards me.

~

# Katy Wimhurst's Biography

Katy Wimhurst read social anthropology before doing research on Mexican surrealism. She has also worked in academic publishing, but now has a chronic illness.

She writes fiction and non-fiction and has been published in various magazines and anthologies, including *The Guardian, The Puritan, To Hull And Back 2017, Black Pear Press, Magic Oxygen Literary Prize* (MOLP4), *Fabula Press, Ouen Press, Patrician Press, Café Irreal, Serendipity, Bust Down the Doors and Eat All the Chickens*, and *The Casket of Fictional Delights*. She won the Earlyworks short story prize 2017 and the Tate Modern short story competition TH2058.

She interviews short story writers for www.theshortstory.co.uk and other literary magazines, and has a particular interest in magical realism and surrealism.

In a past life she might have been Salvador Dali's moustache and she'd like to be reincarnated as one of Russell Hoban's long-lost dreams. She has a soft spot for myth, magic, mongrels and mudflats.

# BUILDING A BRIDGE

*Shortlisted story, by Guy Russell*

It was like being marooned from half the world.

John had two brothers and no sisters. He'd gone to an all-boys school and an all-technology university. His hobbies, unfortunately, were Linux computing, war gaming and Sheffield Wednesday. On finishing his civil engineering degree, he got offered a job in a London consultancy, after which he had only two – not entirely unconnected – goals. Finding accommodation, and… Well, a girlfriend was far beyond his capability. But it was time, it really was overdue time that he had an actual conversation with a woman of his age, or at least exchanged a few words beyond, "A pint of Fullers, please," and, if he was feeling exceptionally bold, "Can you top it up?" to attractive baristas. He was sure he could do it, given the opportunity, in a non-threatening, non-dating, non-stressful environment like a shared kitchen. It couldn't be harder than routing the Normans at Hastings, or installing Flash on 64-bit Ubuntu, or supporting The Owls.

John had friends – male ones – but they were marooned in the same place. Thank heaven for the internet. "Speak softly," it told him. "Don't dominate or be opinionated. Listen a lot. Never talk about, say, Linux distros, cable stay stresses, or medieval battle formations *unless* you're asked about them first, and then don't go on too long, even if they pretend interest. Instead, talk about your feelings, and relationships. Don't sound predatory. Don't sound creepy. Don't make any sexual references whatever. Don't touch them, even slightly. Say 'women', not 'girls'. Be honest. Be tidy. Be considerate. Don't worry if people assume you're gay."

"I'm not gay," slipped out at his first interview, with two women from a shared house in East Reiford. Oh dear, fallen at the first hurdle. Had they thought him homophobic? Overcompensating? Or just predatory?

"I haven't got a girlfriend, but I'm looking for one," escaped accidentally at his second. True, it was honest. It was talking about relationships. But possibly predatory. And a bit creepy.

"I'm not looking for a girlfriend. I just want to be around women," he said at his third. It was perfectly honest. And less predatory. But *extremely* creepy.

He went to other forums. "It doesn't *remotely* matter," the internet told him, "if your housemates think you're sad, square and unmanly. This is a long game. Slowly, you'll be revealing your inner strengths in late-night kitchen heart-to-hearts. *That's* when you shame-dump that you're looking for a girlfriend. Remember, you do *not* want to get off with your housemates. That is *complicated*. You want to be friends with them. What you want is to meet *their* friends."

This was wisdom. Why had he never discovered these sites before?

"We like going out and having fun," he was told after his fourth interview. "You're a bit sad for our house."

"You're slightly too square for us," at his fifth.

"This sounds frightfully odd, and don't take it wrong," said the lasses at his sixth, "but you're not really *manly* enough."

But the seventh was the jackpot. The three women were seemingly as square and sad as he was, and evidently reassured by his crossed legs and muted voice and general non-sexual demeanour. The house, by outer-London rental standards, was almost habitable and almost affordable, and John did more than his share of tidying and, because he couldn't help it, repaired the broken satellite dish and sorted the leak beneath the sink, and soon he was 'sweet' and was having successful conversations about bin-liners and the gas bill and the need to get more milk. When it all got too exhausting, there was always the Linux Computing Meetup or the South Reiford Wargames Society, where he could occasionally say, "My housemate Lucy," or, "My housemate Erica," and be rewarded with a glance of envy.

Work, meanwhile, was going pretty well. It was a relief to switch back into his normal personality, though once or twice he almost crossed his legs. They were trusting him with real structures. He did a commended presentation. He showed his boss a whizzy feature on the AutoCAD.

And then one evening, Lucy came down from her room to make cocoa while he was straightening a cupboard door (he didn't like to hang round the kitchen in case it looked like he wanted to talk, which might seem predatory, but the door had been bothering him).

"You are clever," said Lucy. Then she started telling him about her mum not being well and about her job and John listened a lot and wasn't opinionated, and Lucy stayed at least 20 minutes before going back up.

And the next evening, by coincidence, Erica was cooking real food and offered him some, and actually ignored her phone while she told him how she had two sisters and no brothers and had gone to an all-girls school and then studied nursery nursing, and John listened a lot and wasn't opinionated, and was even quite interested.

And at breakfast the day after that, he bumped into Steph who was up early and talked about Lucy and Erica and their various faults, which surely was very intimate and trusting, and John listened a lot and wasn't opinionated, which was, he decided, exceptionally wise.

Work, meanwhile, was going extremely well. They put him on a road-bridge project. "You're a great team player," said his boss. "I like how you listen properly before you contribute, and don't bluster opinions."

And not long after, the housemates met in the kitchen, and decided they should have a house night out, and pencilled in the following Friday at Fasta Pasta. *Wow*, thought John. He had a social life, with girls in, and it had only taken six months.

*

But Fasta Pasta wasn't a great success. John had a Peroni too many and nearly uncaged his engineering self, and then clammed up in terror. And there was some inexplicable tension between Erica and Steph, and Lucy's tagliatelle wasn't brilliant. Walking home, they all agreed it had been marvellous, in the polite way of lonely people, and that they should do it again. But something in his housemates' undertones told John it wouldn't happen.

His disappointment was partly alleviated the following evening. He accidentally bumped into Erica outside his work, of all places, and she said, "Hey, do you work here?" although he was sure he'd told her not long ago, and she'd been out that way for some not very clear reason but was going home too, and they sat on the tube together and she asked him about building bridges for bypasses, and John talked enough to show he was an open person but not overly. At one point she touched his arm while making a point but he pretended he didn't notice.

And a few days later Lucy amazingly knocked at the door of his room and asked if he could help her move her wardrobe. So he actually went into her room, as if to a foreign country – the family snapshots on the corkboard, the curtains she'd put up, the embroidered cushions, the tidiness… He helped her move the wardrobe and then she kept talking to him and she sat on the bed and he sat cross-legged on an embroidered cushion on the carpet.

"Would you like a glass of wine?" she said.

She went on about her job and her old university. As she topped up his glass, she crouched down and leaned forward on her haunches, and held on to his thigh to steady herself. John decided it was safest to assume she was being informal, and not long afterward he stood up and went, so as not to seem predatory.

And then a few nights after that, John was coming out of the bathroom, wearing only his dressing gown, when he almost bumped into Steph, wearing only an oversized T-shirt, who was directly outside. He was about to move aside when she bent her head forward and, in a confusing, world-disrupting blur, their faces and mouths connected. After an over-long delay, he unclamped his teeth and they stayed that way long enough for his bewilderment to turn to pleasure. Then Steph pulled back and in the blue light of the fire-alarm her smile was the mysterious and fervent one he had seen on adverts. And it was directed at him, so when she took his wrist tightly and led him into her room, he followed like a sheep.

Steph's room was nothing like Lucy's. It was messy and dirty. They hopscotched to the bed over papers and clothes and pizza boxes. Apart from, "I'll put my cap in," and, "No. Like this," and, "Ssshhh," there was no conversation. At five they were woken by her alarm. "Go back to bed," whispered Steph, and he obeyed.

*

John was very happy that morning. Extraordinarily, beamingly happy. People noticed at work. "Wednesday win last night?" said his colleague Dave.

"Get your end away?" said his colleague Steve.

"Fuck off," said John, in his engineering self, still beaming.

It happened again the next night, and the next. *I am*

*having*, thought John, *a sex life*. Which was even better than a social life, wasn't it? Which was, in fact, what a social life was for, wasn't it?

In the night, Steph tapped quietly on his door, and in the kitchen she treated him politely and distantly. It wasn't like lying. It was like acting. Being secretly someone else, a person with a sex life, John felt deep and rich and interesting. But he knew he was a poor actor. He was far too happy. He was far too polite and distant with Steph. Lucy looked at him with a curious air, which changed in a few days to a resigned but smiling air, and was out of the house more often. Erica looked at him with a curious air, which changed in a few days to a disappointed, then a miserable air, and stayed in her room more often, and shortly declared she was looking for somewhere else to live.

"I need to be nearer work," she said, "the commute is too long from here."

"That's a shame," said John. "Stay in touch. I was just beginning to get to know you."

"Likewise," she said.

Work, meanwhile, was going fantastically well. At his appraisal, his boss said he was making a real contribution to the bypass bridge. "You love *things*. You love making things work," he praised. "You're a *real* engineer."

"Thanks," said John.

"But you've also got great personal skills. Which, I can tell you, is rare in this business."

At the interviews for replacing Erica, John liked Sunita but Lucy and Steph liked Ricardo, who was dark-haired and artistic and could talk endlessly about relationships. It was difficult not to be opinionated about him. Then John was away on site for a fortnight, because the bridge's monitoring system had to be tested, and when he came back Steph no longer tapped, and it was like being in withdrawal from an addictive drug. In the kitchen, Steph and Ricardo treated each other politely and distantly. When he imagined saying something, a fat green creature would rise through his throat, watering his eyes.

"And what good would that do?" said the internet. "Let it lie."

Another surprise followed. Lucy became very attractive. Perhaps he had been too unassertive, too unmanly. She had touched his knee once. Perhaps, lustred with his hard-won experience, he should ask her out in the full inverted-commas sense? While he was scrolling the motley opinions, Lucy arrived home with Seamus, whom she'd met on the internet. Seamus was pleasant, softly-spoken and not opinionated, and worked in semiconductor design.

"Cheer up," said the internet. "Take up adult ballet. Join a novel-reading group. Get into knitting or Pilates or crystal healing. Give up your job and become a nursery nurse. Get a house-share with women."

At work, he started loving the bridge. If you got the sums right, it would go up and stay there, and there was something very beautiful about that.

Lucy and Seamus were always in the kitchen now, baking each other cakes and embracing. Steph and Ricardo became openly a couple, which gave them licence to have noisier sex. John re-registered on the house-sharing site. "I need to be nearer work," he said. "The commute's too long from here."

Hey, he realised, Erica. He'd never, considering it dispassionately, had much connection with Steph. It was Erica who'd been like him. And he had her number, somewhere.

They met in a Café Java in New Rigby, further out, where Erica was now living. He had so much to tell her – about Steph, about Ricardo, and about relationships. He was honest but not opinionated. He didn't exactly fancy her – but that would come. Then, before he'd gone on too long, with good conversational manners, John asked about her news. He was still settling to listen when Erica lobbed the word 'boyfriend' across the tea-table. As he rocked from the detonation, John glimpsed her receding into a distant, desirable past. The green creature scrabbled up – but he swallowed it and was polite and congratulatory and, like a friend, invited details. Joseph was gentle, socially-conscious, and worked in a restaurant.

"I'm looking for a girlfriend," John shame-dumped, bravely.

Erica said she didn't know anyone suitable. But what about the internet? "After all," she said, "for an engineer, you're very good at talking to women," and she got out her iPad and there they were, in photos, thousands of them.

"One will do," said John. He had been too unassertive, too unmanly. Between the lines, Joseph sounded opinionated, creepy and quite unsuitable. Erica *was* the one. He could have conversations with her. He could be open and honest. It was time to be spontaneous. "Just one," he said. "You, for instance."

"John," said Erica, "haven't you been *listening*? I have a boyfriend. And I really must go now."

Blast, blast. Predatory, predatory. Why was it so difficult? Why?

Why?

Work, meanwhile, was going utterly brilliantly. The

project completed on time, on budget and with style. The traffic crossed the bridge and zoomed off, sending exhaust fumes and tail-lights into the sunset. There was a big formal celebration and afterwards, the pub. His boss put a tab behind the bar. Steve, Dave, the boss and the whole team got steadily noisier. Mildly drunk, and high on praise, John went up to the bar.

"A pint of Fullers please," he said to the attractive barista, and a minute later, because he was feeling exceptionally bold, "Can you top it up?"

"There you go," she said. "What are you all celebrating over there?"

"We've built a bridge," said John. "And it still hasn't fallen down."

She gave a laugh. John paused a moment. Then grandly, ruggedly, swayingly, like a man who has really achieved something, he began carrying his beer back to his table.

~

## Guy Russell's Biography

Guy Russell was born in Chatham and has been a holiday courier, purchasing clerk, media analyst and fan-heater production operative. He currently lives in Milton Keynes.

Work in *Brace* (Comma), *Troubles Swapped For Something Fresh* (Salt), *Madame Morte* (Black Shuck), *The Iron Book of New Humorous Verse* (Iron), *Flash 500*, *Liars' League* and elsewhere.

# DIGI-MAN

*Shortlisted story, by Jonathan Macho*

Cardiff Council HQ, 202X. After the Tweet Cascade of 201X cripples the world, unparalleled efficiency is required to restore order. Software is developed to ensure it will never slip again.

Digital Manager. Digiman for short. Brevity is efficient, after all.

Unbeknownst to its creators, Digiman's title will soon pass from machine, to man, to legend.

This is that legend.

\*

Digiman monitored conversation, November 1st, 202X. Efficiency rating: 49.00%

"You listening, Andrews?"

"Yes, sir. Every word."

"Good. I don't like having to repeat myself. Ever. Repetition is inefficient, as you well know."

"Yes, sir. You've told me often enough."

"Hm. Yes. Anyway, this software, Digiman as it's called, will be a crucial part of your job going forward. It's a straightforward thing, all told, but it will be crucial in making sure you're doing all you need to be. It's crucial you're up to speed with how it all works, crucial."

"Yes, sir, I was getting that."

"As I say, it's not going to be a strain on you. No more than the work you do already, anyway. You simply log in when you arrive in the morning, like so, then click out for the duration of your 15 minute mandatory-by-law lunch break, and then again when you head home. The Digiman's clock counts every nanosecond you're at your workstation, and every nanosecond you're not. That way, we can be aware that you're doing everything you're supposed to when you're supposed to be doing it. And it's a faultless system, so I'm told. Faultless. Your time will never be wasted again. We've made sure of that. Very helpful of us, eh?"

"Very."

"I think we deserve a 'thank you', Andrews. I think considering we, the leaders of the council, are going to such effort to make sure you are operating at maximum efficiency, not to mention in a way that is entirely without fault, the least you can do is show some gratitude."

"..."

"Don't keep us waiting, Andrews. Waiting is inefficiency personified."

"Thank you, sir."

"Oh, don't thank me Andrews. Thank Digiman."

"..."

"I wasn't being rhetorical."

"Thank you... Digiman."

"Splendid. Well, that's enough time wasted on learning. There's important work to be done, always is. So remember – and you better, Andrews – I'm never repeating it. Clock in, clock out. Simple stuff. See you later."

"OK, but, sir... Sir? Oh, he's gone. He never showed me how to clock out. Well, looks like he's logged me in anyway, so all I need to figure out is... Sod it, I've got actual work to do. Just remember to puzzle it out before I head home..."

*

And so, software is born. Gripping.

The story now jumps forward six months, to show what comes of this interaction. This is because to continue in real time would be ridiculously inefficient.

*

Lloyd Andrews was heading home when the man in the lion skin threw a spear at his head.

He was making his way between two of the endless building sites that peppered the city, wondering for the millionth time if they were ever going to be completed, when he saw a gleam somewhere high in the scaffolds. He thought about how depressingly efficient the builders were, up there at this hour, but the gleam was growing and it was heading his way. Squealing, he fell on his backside and felt the air cleave where his head had been seconds before. He turned, watching the spear skid along the pavement behind him, then looked back in time to see a man spring from the girders above and land gracefully a few feet away.

No matter how impressive an entrance that was, the figure the man cut was more daft than anything else. He had a thick black moustache, handlebars Lloyd believed, and a mane of black hair slicked back from his face. This was not his only mane however — draped over his shoulders were billowing furs, fastened onto what could have been a lion-skin waistcoat. His trousers were patterned like cheetah skin, or leopard maybe, and his belt was striped like a zebra. It was the ugliest get-up Lloyd had ever seen, glaringly bright even on this grey afternoon. If he'd seen the man walking down St Mary's Street, he might have suppressed a laugh, or winced.

The spear on the ground and the knives in his hands put paid to that reaction, however.

"I am Cra'van the hunter," the man screamed in a thick accent, "and you are my prey."

"I'm sorry," Lloyd coughed. "Craven, was it?"

"Cra'van," the man insisted. "It is a small, but important difference."

"OK, Mr... Cra'van, I think you've mistaken me for someone else. My name is Lloyd. Lloyd Andrews. Hello." Lloyd gave a little wave.

Cra'van spat on the ground. "There is no mistaking," he snarled, advancing slowly, playing with the knives as he went. "You are the one who is worthy of my attentions. You are the superhuman who has drawn me here."

"Superhuman?" Lloyd laughed this time, and immediately regretted it. "Oh no, sir, you're definitely wrong there. I'm just a scanner, from Penylan. Nothing remotely super about me."

"I admit," the hunter mused, keeping pace with Lloyd as he wiggled back along the concrete, "you are not what I expected. I am surprised you do not work, even now, as your reputation states. However, your record remains unparalleled. As soon as it came to my attention, I knew that you were to be my first superhuman quarry. That you would be enough of a challenge for Cra'van."

"Record?" Lloyd blinked. "What record?"

Cra'van stopped and sniffed. Lloyd did the same on reflex and gagged. The man smelt worse than the office food waste bin. "You try to lure me into trap. I see now. No way a man of your reputation this easy to cage." He threw a knife into the air and caught it again, like a kid with a tennis ball. Lloyd squeaked and waved his arms wildly. "No way any man this easy to cage. I..."

Suddenly he stiffened, alert. Twisting on the spot, he took in all directions. "A pack? Why would you have need of a pack?"

Lloyd had no idea what he was talking about, but that was nothing new.

Cra'van turned on him, eye's blazing. "I am ill prepared, but will not underestimate you again." Before any response was offered, he vaulted over Lloyd's shaking form, sprinted to collect his spear and vanished into the shadows of a refurbishing shopping centre.

Lloyd stared after him, more confused than he'd ever been in his life. He was about to take a breath when a bag was pulled over his head and he was dragged away.

\*

We now jump forward again, but only into the afternoon.

If the pace of this legend alarms you at any point, please take solace in the fact that such speed is highly efficient, and therefore encouraged under law.

\*

When the bag was finally pulled away, Lloyd found himself in a cavernous room. It looked to him like a cathedral, grand and ornate, but it was still under construction. Scaffolds dotted the roof and a 'Hard Hats Must Be Worn' sign hung from an altar. It was both reassuring and alarming. Then, a yellow safety helmet was placed on him by shaking hands; the same hands that had bundled him into the car that had brought him wherever the hell this was. Behind the altar stood a woman in a flowing green robe, arms spread, grinning wildly.

"Lo, the Digi-man has come," she cried. "Praise him."

Lloyd jumped out of his skin as the room chorused, "DIGI-MAN, DIGITAL MANAGER, DIGI-MAN IS OUR CHAMPION." He hadn't noticed the massive congregation that filled the space, each in their own green robes and hard hats. He'd only just had his bag removed, to be fair.

The woman made her way towards him. "Welcome to our humble church, Lord."

First superhuman, now lord? He must have been

looking sharp today. "What's going on?" he managed after a moment. "Are you with that nut in the lion skin?"

"Oh no," she said quickly, obviously appalled at the idea. "Cra'van is a faithless thing. He was once a big game hunter, but the great efficacy drive of the last decade led to him hunting many animals to extinction. Now it seems he has targeted you. As soon as we were aware, we knew we must act to protect you."

Even after all that, Lloyd was none the wiser. "And you are?"

"I am Bishop Jasmine, and we are the Church of the Digi-man."

"DIGI-MAN, DIGITAL MANAGER, DIGI-MAN IS OUR CHAMPION."

Lloyd jumped again at the mantra. There really were a lot of them, weren't there? And there it was again. Did they mean the thing from work? "So…" He scratched his head. "You all work for the council?"

"Of course not," she said. "I mean… some of us do. Jan, Ben, you work for the council, right?" There was muffled assent from one of the pews in the back.

"But then… why are you talking about their software?" Lloyd felt like there were some better question to be asked, but he wanted to get this one out of the way. "Are you thinking of installing it here? I'm not really the right person to talk to."

"You are confused, Lord," Jasmine sighed, pityingly. Even when he was a 'lord' people seemed to feel sorry for him. "That is understandable. We acted rashly in your retrieval, but we wanted to get you to safety as soon as possible. I'm sure with your record, you would have handled the whole thing a lot more efficiently."

"That guy said the same thing. What record? I don't

have any record."

Jasmine blinked. "Your record for the most consecutive hours worked by any human being in history, as recorded on your namesake."

Lloyd went cold. "What did you say?"

"It currently stands at 4,389 hours, 17 minutes, 11 seconds and 108 nanoseconds," she continued. "This has become commonly acknowledged as more than any mortal could withstand. An efficiency beyond efficiency."

"Oh God... I never turned my Digiman off," Lloyd breathed. "Do you know what this means?"

"Of course," Jasmine said simply. "You are our one true lord and saviour, come to show us all the path to peak productivity."

Lloyd went colder. "Excuse me?"

"Now, some would try and remove such a positive figure for progress. The slovenly and the afraid will not allow you to live and continue your good, endless work..."

Colder still. "EXCUSE ME?"

"But you are safe here, Lord," she insisted. "Nothing may harm you within these walls."

That was when the gunfire started. Men dressed all in black burst through the church's windows and kicked down its doors, rifles raised, barking orders. Everyone started screaming and just as Lloyd decided to join in, another bag was over his head and he was gone.

*

You may consider the number of times bags are pulled over Lloyd's head on this fateful day noteworthy. Such acts are fairly common in 202X, however. Explaining why you need someone to come with you eats up valuable time. Time Digi-man no longer has.

*

When he came to he was strapped to a cold metal table in a stark white room. There was an observation window built into the one wall he could see and, standing behind it, was his line manager, Samuel Stern. He was living up to his namesake, sporting that kind of expression that said a team meeting full of passive aggressive judging was on the cards. Lloyd couldn't give a monkey's by this point, frankly. He'd had enough.

"Sir?" he tried weakly. "Sam, is that you?"

"Hello, Lloyd," Stern said in the least friendly way possible. "How are you?"

"Not good," Lloyd said after a while. "I've had a really bad day."

"So I hear. Hunted by a madman, kidnapped by your own church..." Stern massaged his brow like this was all very irritating for him. Not for the first time, Lloyd wanted to throw him off of something. "We acted on it all as soon as we knew, but everything happens so quickly these days... The one downside to efficiency."

"So you know about my Digiman?" Despite himself, Lloyd felt awkward. He knew a bollocking was coming for his admin error. "I'm really sorry about that. I just forgot to clock out at the end of the day."

"Well, it's not quite just that, is it, Lloyd?" Stern said in that condescending way of his. "You forgot to clock out six months ago. Our infallible system has been recording you as at your desk, working hard, since I first logged you in. You have the record for longest unceasing work day by over 4,000 hours. Not only that, we're in trouble with the unions for denying you six months' worth of mandatory-by-law lunch breaks."

"But I had those lunch breaks. I just didn't click out when..."

"We know that, Lloyd," Stern snapped. "We just can't admit it."

Lloyd frowned. "What do you mean?" When no answer came, he added, "Look, I'll explain it, just unstrap me and..." Lloyd suddenly and horribly remembered he was strapped to a table. "Sir, why am I here?"

"For the dissection, of course."

Lloyd was in freefall. "What? What dissection?"

"As I said," Stern grumbled, obviously irked to be repeating himself, "you are recorded as having the longest work day of any council employee. Obviously, your inhuman feat merits further study. Your body may hold the key to improving our efficiency a thousand fold. Therefore, the leaders have approved your educational dismemberment at our earliest convenience."

Lloyd couldn't think straight. Hadn't he just said...? "You just said," he blurted. "You just said you knew the reason why. I'm not a superman, or a Digi-man, or whatever. I just didn't know how to click out. I told you."

"And I told you, many times, the Digiman system is completely without fault. Admitting that you are inefficient, by extension, admits that we are wrong. Too many people know about you now, people we have promised that Digiman is flawless. It makes more sense to agree that you are special and dispose of you forthwith, than to break our promises and find a whole new system."

"You're killing me, cutting me apart, and you know it's for no reason? But that's insane."

Stern sighed. "No, it is simply efficient."

\*

The council scrambled, hurrying back and forth, tripping over themselves in a most unproductive manner. To save face, to save the system, the man had to die. In their blinkered, unruly hurry, however, they had forgotten one crucial piece of the puzzle, one flaw they had not foreseen, still ticking in the background.

If Digi-man was dead, then why was his clock still going?

If nobody remembered to click him off, what kind of legend would he yet become?

~

## Jonathan Macho's Biography

Jonathan Macho is a Scanner/Writer who lives in Cardiff with his family, his neighbour's cat and a seriously legit talking space raccoon.

He's been published in quite a few short story anthologies now, including two prior To Hull And Back humour anthologies from 2015 and 2016 and the first and third issues of 404 INK's literary magazine.

His short story 'The Two Brigadiers' was given to subscribers of the Lethbridge-Stewart range and can be read for free as part of The Lucy Wilson Collection, found online at: www.candy-jar.co.uk/books/avatarsof theintelligence.html

He has also had short plays put on by the Sherman

Youth Theatre in Cardiff and been shortlisted in the Terry Hetherington Young Writer's Award 2017. Some days, he scans things too.

# DREAM INTERRUPTED

*Shortlisted story, by Katie Burton*

I'm in the middle of the best dream I've ever had when I accidentally wake up. For a few seconds I refuse to accept it. I say to my brain, *Back to sleep now little one, sleepy time now, la la la la la, one, two, three, four sheep.*

OK, I'm definitely awake. And I need a wee.

As Dad says, *a lot*, life is unfair.

But I choose not to listen to old Papa. He is a pessimist to the extreme. Why should life be so unfair? As I said to him over breakfast the other day, "Father, I am going to have a fabulous life. There's nothing you can say that will persuade me otherwise."

He just raised his eyebrows and carried on listening to *The Archers* on the radio. He is very old and grumpy. He thinks he knows all the sadness of life. He thinks, and I know this because he has told me on numerous occasions, that I am 'unrealistic' and that I 'expect too much for too little'.

So, anyway, back to this dream. I am sitting on the loo with my eyes shut. My thinking is, if I keep them shut it will be easier to fall back to sleep and get back into the dream. Then I'll find out how it finishes and discover the path to true happiness and bliss etc.

It isn't that easy, weeing with your eyes shut, as I discover when I stand up and knock the toilet roll into the toilet bowl. I only know this has happened because I hear a splash. But que sera sera, as some jolly old blonde once sung. I shall deal with it in the morning.

Now, snoozy snoozy, back to sleep. Back to dreams.

*

My alarm goes off for school and for a moment I am as bleary-eyed as a mole. Then I remember. Even though I am me, and I strive to be a glass-half-full-at-all-times kind of girl, so that I don't ever turn into Daddio, I am disappointed. I did not re-enter the most amazing dream that has ever been dreamed. Instead, I dreamt about splashing around in a toilet bowl.

But let no one say I'm a quitter. I shall simply get my

dream back. I tell Dad this at brekkie. "I've got to rush out before school because I'm going to get a dream back that I only got halfway through," I say, through a mouthful of shredded wheat. Not ladylike, I know, but time waits for no woman.

"Sounds like a lot of effort for a dream," he says.

I explain, very patiently, that it was a super-duper dream and that, if only I can get to the end, my whole life will change because the dream was about to show me how to become rich and famous. I grin a very charming grin, just to demonstrate my potential for fame and fortune. I may have shredded wheat stuck in my teeth, but still.

"Maybe you should spend the time revising for your maths exam instead," says Dad. "Unless you want to end up unemployed and destitute. Like your brother."

He is so unimaginative. You would almost think he wants me to have a horrible life. I say this to him. "Do you want me to have a horrible life?"

He eats a spoonful of peanut butter out of the jar — he is revolting. "Not at all, darling. I just think the sooner you learn that life is a pain in the arse from start to finish, the better."

Honestly, it's a miracle I have managed to cling on to such a sunny disposition.

He also says, "Did you drop a toilet roll in the loo and leave it for me to fish out?" but I am far too busy for such trivial matters. I run upstairs, stuff all my things into my bag and leap back down two at a time.

I am bounding out the door when Dad calls after me. "Take a coat."

"Why?" I shout back. "It's lovely and sunny. It's a beautiful day to be alive."

*

I am sopping wet in my summer dress. It is stuck to my legs like sausages in cling film. A man in a van honks his horn. But still, I am youthful and in my prime. Honk away, you old paedo. I skip along for all the world to admire, despite the fact I have squelchy knickers.

At the pharmacy, I say to the lady, "I need something to help get a dream back. You see, I was only half way through a dream when I woke up, and I need to finish it off."

It's all raised eyebrows and head shaking. Her bob bobs about. She looks overly alarmed for a lady who spends her days dealing with old people's crusty skin complaints. "Oh no, I don't recommend that at all. It's never a good idea to go back to a dream. They usually finish when they do for a very good reason."

I smile patiently. It may be that one day I become the Prime Minister and I shall be required to deploy this smile all the time.

"I realise that is the case most of the time," I say. "But this is a special case. You see, this dream was meant to be finished."

"That would be unusual. What happened in the dream?"

"Oh, well, it's a bit hard to explain."

"You'll need to try."

I feel a bit embarrassed actually, which is unlike me. "Well, I was in a forest and there was this guy with super long, blond hair and pointy ears. He was sitting on a unicorn with a rainbow mane and he was just *lovely*. I was about to get on stage to sing a song I had written – I was going to win this huge singing contest. Anyway, this guy with the unicorn starts telling me how successful I am going to be and that, if I only listen carefully, I can learn how to make all my dreams come true. I mean, he was literally about to tell me the secrets of fame and fortune. Then, just as he started, I woke up."

There are mutters from behind me now and Mrs Pharmacist looks cross. A rowdy kid tries to swipe a lollypop from the counter and she bats him away – not a lover of children, evidently. Or teenagers it would seem. Calmly, I continue to explain the situation. My powers of persuasion are really top notch. Also, I go on and on and on and on.

"After all," I say finally, throwing my hands into the air. "What is life without a dream?"

*

I wrap the little bottle carefully in my cardie and carry it around all day. I am so excited. I will probably never get to sleep so I rush about more than usual to tire myself out. I do 100 jumping jacks in the corridor as we wait to go into the maths exam. People stare, but I suppose I should get used to attention. The exam is not what you would call a roaring success, but you have to prioritise to be successful in life. I have chosen not to prioritise maths.

*

I run around all evening. Dad is lounging on the sofa watching something about cars. He just raises his eyebrows when I run into the living room, do five press-ups, then run out again. Until the fifth time I do this, when he tells me to, "Sit the hell down." We watch a depressing drama about war and people dying and stuff.

"See, my dear," says Dad, stretching his hands above his head. "Life is hard, and then you die."

\*

I am tired out although still excited of course. In my room I pull out the little bottle. The liquid inside is thick, like a smoothie, but it doesn't taste like a smoothie unless they make them out of mud and liquorice now. Quite, quite disgusting. Such is the price for my beautiful dream.

I poke my head around Dad's door and say goodnight before I get into bed. "So tonight's the night is it?" he says. "The dream to end all dreams shall finally be dreamed?"

I just smile. I won't rise to his sarcastic ways, they are truly the tool of a very sad, old person. Now, snuggle snuggle, down into my bed of dreams. Lights off and falling, falling...

Oh it's so lovely here. A dappled forest, a shaded clearing. There's the unicorn and the man with flowing hair coming towards me. Quite a lot like Legolas from *The Lord of the Rings* films. In fact, now I'm back, it might actually be Legolas from *The Lord of the Rings* films. We sit down by a pool. A waterfall cascades just to our right, sending rainbows dancing all around because, ah yes, I remember now, the rocks are all crystals. I am looking super. My skin is clear, all my spots are gone, my hair is longer. I am about to perform a song for a huge crowd, but first I must hear what Legolas has to say because it will change my life forever.

He's talking now, softly. He's telling me that I have

so much potential and that I am totally right to be optimistic about the future because all I need to do to become rich and famous is...

Ouch.

What on earth?

I am on the floor. Literally, I am on the floor of my room. How did I end up here? I close my eyes and get back into dream world. Where was I?

Oh... Oh no... I remember.

Legolas was just about to speak, just about to tell me the secret of everlasting success, when he sneezed. His unicorn with the rainbow mane reared up in fright and kicked him in the head. He came bowling towards me, I rolled out the way as fast as I could and now...

Yes. I am on the floor. I have bruised my bottom.

There are hurried footsteps and Dad is at the door. He looks worried. For a millisecond. Then he figures out what has happened.

I get back into bed with dignity and pull the cover up to my chin as Dad practically pees himself with laughter. The word 'guffaw' comes to mind. *Come on now*, I tell myself, *don't be ridiculous, there's no reason to cry*.

I listen to Dad stumbling back to bed. Through the wart-hoggy snorts I hear him say, "And that... just goes to show... life really is... a pain in the bum."

I sniff and burrow into the duvet. I hate to say it, but for once in his life, he might have a point.

~

## Katie Burton's Biography

Katie Burton is a Londoner through and through. Having graduated from UCL with a BA in history and no idea what to do next, she worked in an old-fashioned sweet shop before making the grave error of becoming a corporate solicitor.

Last year, she got married, quit her job, re-trained as a journalist and now writes whatever she can, for whoever she can.

Her proudest achievement is proposing to her now-husband on the top of a mountain in a fit of feminism and gin.

She writes book reviews of fantasy literature at www.fantasyliterature.com/author/katie-burton/ and she writes a blog:

www.nothingifnotahypocrite.blogspot.com

# HUMBLE BEGETTINGS

*Shortlisted story, by Leema Ahmed*

"The pregnancy test was negative, I'm afraid." I broke the sad news to the IVF nurse in a calm but sympathetic voice. I spent a couple of minutes consoling her about the failed implantation before moving on to provide hope for future attempts. She seemed a little thrown off at the role reversal. This routine I repeated with our family and a few close friends, determined to corral my own miserable feelings.

Within two days, the physical aftermath of the IVF was too overwhelming to leave room for sulking. Over the week, my side of the bed came to resemble the bloody murder bed from a homicide investigation drama. Sleep disappeared whilst I endeavoured to battle horrible pains and various other objectionable symptoms. I developed the bedraggled and crazed aspect of a natural born killer, a million miles from the soft glow and eyes-twinkling-with-secret-life look that I had been gunning for that week. And to put the icing on the bodily indignities cake, I developed a haemorrhoid. A little, round nuisance which I understood often developed following the hefty doses of injected hormones.

Initially, it only showed itself on bathroom visits. But then one night, it made its foray into outdoor living whilst I was lying innocently in bed. I was most annoyed by this new and unnatural sensation. To top it off, my phone had just pinged with a message from a friend's partner, thanking us for our housewarming gifts. His name was Miles. This had never been an issue before, but somehow in my sleepy, drug-addled state my desire to respond well to the social overture from Miles became confused with my desire to respond adequately to my new problem of piles, and I dreamt strange dreams of polite conversation with my haemorrhoid.

My review with the IVF consultant came round. By then I was feeling human again, except that the haemorrhoid seemed to be on the up despite my efforts with steroid cream. I gave the consultant my usual encouraging patter, and he nodded sympathetically as he'd heard it all before. When I told him I was physically more or less recovered other than the pile, I was dismayed to be asked to pop on the couch. A nurse was called in, and after the basic prodding examination, I was told they were just getting the ultrasound to have a closer look.

*What fresh hell is this now?* I thought. There were

the lubricated manoeuvrings of the scanner, a few captured stills and a whispered conversation between the clinicians, during which I could have sworn I heard the phrase, "Foetal sac."

Back at the desk my gynaecologist said, "Well it appears you have a condition known as gravidum ectopia asinum." He explained that whilst it was common knowledge that ectopic pregnancies could occur in the fallopian tubes, an extremely rare other site was the lower part of the rectum. He paused to let this sink in.

Uncertain whether to be overjoyed or disgusted, a curious affective dilemma, I clarified, "So I am pregnant?" to which he smiled and congratulated us.

From his shelf he pulled down a journal, *Annales d'obstétrique et de gynécologie*, and leafed through the pages 'til he arrived at a moody calotype of a woman in a Victorian style bodice and long skirt with full and rounded bustle. To my astonishment, the next photograph showed the woman disrobed, and that the 'bustle', instead of being formed by horsehair petticoats, had been shaped by a large, fleshy egg shape that protruded from her behind. I felt a little nauseated.

"You should be alright," said my doctor, "as long as you do your pelvic floor exercises."

The first trimester advanced with much of the usual cocktail of sickness, exhaustion and bra buying. Accommodating the awkward bump was my own peculiar challenge and I found myself returning to the IVF nurse for advice. This time I embraced my role as 'worried mother-to-be', but the poor nurse was doomed to remain stuck firmly outside her comfort zone with me. The baby scans too were unorthodox. In my starring role I had fancied myself lying comfortably in a cosy pastel top, flushed face turned expectantly towards the monitor, hand in my husband's, as gel was squirted onto my smooth and sublimely rotund tummy. Instead, the scans were done in doggy position and I was supremely grateful not to have to look the technician in the eye.

By the latter half of the pregnancy, mobility became challenging and I was forced to take leave from work early. This left me with plenty of time for dawdling on our High Street looking at the maternity outfits that I would have worn. During my IVF trials I had often envisioned proudly bearing my baby bump into public spaces, the exemplar of self-satisfied fecundity. Instead as I John-Wayned it awkwardly down the High Street, no older women fluttered excitedly to my side with questions of due dates. Even the *Big Issue* vendors avoided me. And certainly, no friend or family ever asked to feel the baby kicking.

The 'egg', in due course, completely obscured my out passage, so that most of our nutrition had to be provided intravenously. I became weary of hearing, "You're not very generous today, are you?" from scolding district nurses who'd failed to cannulate me. So much for giving into weird food cravings. At this rate I would have no zany anecdotes at all. As for the permissible, no, *praiseworthy* eating for two that I'd been looking forward to, this little arsehole baby was preventing me from eating at all.

My last pregnancy dream to bite the dust was the one where I would paint or, in more advanced fantasies, stencil a nursery. I had looked forward to perversely taking my centre of gravity challenged body up a ladder to paint a nursery ceiling, as this seemed to me to be some kind of dangerous rite of passage, modern pregnancies being perhaps too simple and safe to suffice. Unfortunately, I fell at the first hurdle, being unable to even pull up a pair of painterly dungarees. Instead, the last weeks found me sitting quietly, cross legged around the egg, my roosting meditations interrupted only by the baby repeatedly kicking my backside.

On the due date, eight months after the faux haemorrhoid's presentation, my family, the clinical team and I were on tenterhooks. The surgery went smoothly and I was delivered safely of a healthy baby daughter. When the theatre nurse handed me our precious brat, her eyes shone with triumph. We too could hardly believe our luck, and how perfect our diminutive progeny was, as she lay sleepily oblivious to her own very singular incubation.

Recollections of our uncertain and frequently humiliating journey to parenthood are fading fast. Partly, this is due to exhaustion from the baby's constant needs, which no forewarning had apparently prepared us for. Partly because every time she squirms for comfort on our shoulders, directs a gummy smile at us, or does any number of similarly stupendous things, the memory of those difficulties lose some of their definition.

The fever dream has finally broken to a bright and new reality. I wonder what will happen next time.

~

# Leema Ahmed's Biography

I am a Mancunian who went to London for medical school and then came back, fiancé in tow, to finish my training as an older adults' psychiatrist. I have also completed a Masters in mental health law, a related area that I am quite interested in.

This is my first foray into creative writing. I am so far genre neutral, though an element of silliness seems always to pollute my ponderings. My ambition is to write about the kind of things that cause pain and explore them in a way that makes them lighter.

# MIRACLES, MERCIES AND MARY... ON TOAST

*Shortlisted story, by Sherry Morris*

We live in one of those heartland towns where there's five times as many churches as schools. Even so, *Miracle* wasn't my first thought when my husband, Bobby, announced he was having religious visions. God knows the word was *simulacrum*. Followed by wondering if he'd seen a Jesus Nebula, Nun Bun, or the rarely-seen Virginal Veggie Pizza.

He'd walked in, holding his John Deere cap in both hands, his face shining like the girls' on Christmas morning. He seemed to float across the kitchen to a chair.

"What?" I said, helping him sit down.

"Mary's come to me. With a plan."

"Your sister?" I asked. "What's she doing in the fields?"

"No. *The Virgin Mary*. She smells of roses."

I have a confession to make. *Simulacrum* wasn't the first thought that came to me. That came later, after contemplation, and help from the internet. My real first thought was to call the doctor. I'd heard people smelled roses right before they died.

"Stay still, Bobby." I said. "You might be having a stroke."

"No, hun," Bobby said, taking my hand. "She's been talking to me in the tractor. For a while. She didn't want me to tell anyone, not even you, but now I'm going public. I said I'd speak to you first."

I looked at my husband of 10 years. I'd known him since childhood. I examined his face, his eyes, wished I could see into his heart. Or better yet, his head.

"You're saying the Mother of Jesus Christ Our Lord, has been visiting you in your tractor cab?"

"Uh-huh. She wants me to start preaching at the church now — there's more space."

We'd had our ups and downs, me and Bobby, but he was a good man. A kind, caring man. With a big heart. Sometimes I wished his brain was as big as his heart, but we all do the best we can with what we have.

"How about meeting here in the kitchen first? Invite family and friends. See what happens? We could get a few more chairs."

Bobby let go of my hand.

"There's no need to meet in the kitchen. It'll happen. At church."

He'd always had a strong, quiet faith. That's what made him a decent man and a catch for this town. Most guys had descended into drugs. Others joined the priesthood or military. Some just drove away. Bobby chose to help run our family farm. I guess I should have sent up a prayer of thanks, but I thanked the stars above instead. Sure, it meant I stayed here. But I didn't mind. Most days. It'd been hard when my best friend, Rae, went off to study astronomy. First female in our town to be awarded a full science scholarship. That was something to be proud of. No point dwelling on the fact there'd been two places available.

These days, my thoughts barely wandered to the sky. I was rooted to family and farm. Then Bobby had his encounter with the heavens.

"Bobby, how'd ya know it's the Virgin Mary talking to you? Did she show ID? Wow you with her bible verses? Did she swear that conception was immaculate?"

Bobby shook his head.

"She said you'd doubt. She knows about you. The things you hold sacred – black holes, cosmic rays, the Kirkwood gap. You can't see those things, but you believe they're there. I hear you talking to the girls."

That made me blink. I hadn't realised Bobby had been listening.

"I'm not doubting you exactly," I said. We'd both learned about the sacred visitations at Fatima and Lourdes in school. It'd be difficult to argue against these teachings. But they could work in my favour.

"It's just that the Holy Mother tends to visit children herding sheep. Not grown men in tractor cabs..."

He looked at me, trying to work out if I was poking fun. I wasn't sure myself.

"Tell me everything," I said. "From the beginning."

*

She'd visited him daily for the past six months, giving him bible passages to read and interpret, prayers to say, and deeds to perform, like visiting the sick and laying flowers on graves. He'd passed all her tests and earned himself a hero halo.

Now she wanted him to lead a monthly three-hour prayer service at the church where the annual Crowning of The Virgin took place. He also talked about preaching tours. He'd start small – travelling to neighbouring communities, but this could grow into trips to other states, or even abroad with shows involving him and his tractor, the cab filled with roses. I let him talk, wondering if he was listening to himself.

*

In some ways, finding out what was going on was a relief. Bobby had been getting up extra early in the mornings and taking off in his truck. My wife's mind said *farm work*. But my woman's mind had whispered *affair*. This was something else entirely. Sort of. My husband was being visited privately by a woman – maybe not a breathing one, but her ever-virginal body had been wholly assumed into Heaven and was now, apparently, appearing before him. His heart and mind were full of her. She was taking his time and taking him away from me and the girls. Just like a mistress would. After he finished talking, I said the only thing I could that wouldn't start a fight.

"I need time to think... and pray."

"Sure," Bobby said. "It's a lot to take in."

"What about the farm?" I asked. "Me and Dad can't do it all."

"We're moving. To the church grounds."

"We are?" I said.

"There's a trailer we'll use. The Blessed Virgin's got it all worked out."

"Does she now..." I said.

He looked at the calendar.

"We have eight days," he said, explaining the service would take place on the 13th of every month to guarantee our safety.

"Safety," I said. "From what?"

"Tornadoes," Bobby replied solemnly. "She's promised that if we have this procession each month, no tornado will ever hit the town."

"I see," was all I could say.

"Pretty good deal, don't you think?"

When I didn't respond, he kissed the top of my head and returned to his tractor cab. And her.

I poured myself a coffee and tried to organise my thoughts. It seemed I was now pitted against an entity who moved within the inner circle of Heaven's Holy Trinity. How could I compete with that? Did Victoria's Secret carry a suitable angel outfit? I doubted it. And it was clear devilry playing the natural disaster card. We were at the mercy of tornados every spring, heading to the basement for protection, sometimes spending the night hunched together in the dark around a radio. The destruction they caused was real. Unlike these visitations, I suspected. But saying that wouldn't solve anything. I couldn't let this uproot my family. I needed some intervention from people who'd see my side of the situation. Better yet if they held some divine authority in Bobby's eyes. It came to me as a revelation: the town's Chamber of Commerce. It was run by a group of professional women. They'd be sympathetic and objective. They definitely carried weight – they ran the largest monthly church bingo in five counties.

*

They listened attentively while I talked and clucked their tongues in sympathy.

"We see your dilemma, Grace," Peggy, the chairwoman said. "But look at the bigger picture. When the Rapture comes, your family will be sitting pretty... Perhaps you'll consider putting in a good word for the Chamber... and the Benevolent Ladies of the Blessed Bingo Club."

Adele added, "We've just had the bingo hall repainted, Grace. It'd be a real shame to have it blow away. The whole town would be grateful, knowing their homes were safe because of you. You'd be voted resident of the year... Every year."

I looked around the table at the women, all nodding their heads in agreement.

"So you think this is real?" I asked.

They shrugged. The bottom line was religious sightings were good for business. They provided buzz, publicity and, as an afterlife bonus, brought favour with the Lord.

"You might even get a reality show out of it," Shirley advised. "She is, after all, an A-lister. If it turns out to be a hoax or she stops appearing, you can always go back to your lives."

But I wasn't sure we could.

I called Rae in Arizona – that was where the best

went to work in space science. She listened without interrupting.

"Come for a visit," she said. "No tornados here. Just lizards and prickly pears. I'd get you into the observatory. Looking up at stars instead of down at hymnals."

I sighed. Rae heard everything I couldn't say in that sigh.

"Alright, here's what you do. Stay on the farm with the girls. Let him move to the trailer for his prayer gigs."

That sounded vaguely feasible. She added, "Maybe he'll tire from it. Or you will… You know what to do, Grace. You just want someone else to say it."

I hung up quickly then. In case she said it.

*

So we stayed on the farm and Bobby moved to the trailer. It was a compromise as delicate as a Communion wafer. I tried to convince myself it would work. I realised it wouldn't when I found myself in an armchair, sporting a baseball helmet and a catcher's mask in that godforsaken trailer, while Bobby sat on the sofa, drinking a beer.

"It's not gonna hit," he said, patting my shoulder. "It was sweet of you to stop by, but She's promised. You'll see – This Too Shall Pass."

I'd come to take him to the basement at the farm. At least during the storm. I didn't want my girls to grow up without a daddy – even one a bit touched. But he wouldn't budge. Said I needed to have faith, that this was all part of Her plan. The two of them would help me find my faith and stop tearing our family apart.

"You gotta be willing to sacrifice," he said, shaking

his head.

As if I hadn't known that already.

I got mad as hell then. At him, me. Her. But it was too late to leave the trailer. Tornados picked up cars and tossed them like toys. I had to stay. I found rope and tied myself to the armchair, strapped on the baseball helmet, put on the catcher's mask.

Bobby watched from the sofa.

"You're crazy," he said, then went back to his beer. It came to me then, a way to take the smug look off his face, maybe even get him to take the situation seriously.

"You're not protected."

He sighed. "If only you'd believe in the right higher power. Your twinkly stars and asteroids can't help you now."

"The trailer and church sit outside the city limits."

His face became puzzled. "What?"

"She said a tornado wouldn't hit the town, right?"

"Yes."

"Check an ordnance map. We're outside town."

He paused, blinked a few times, shook his head.

"Nah, doesn't work like that. I'll smell the roses and it'll be alright."

But a look of doubt crossed his face.

I leaned towards him as far as the rope would allow.

"If the tornado hits and we survive, Bobby, you'll stop this and come back to us and the farm."

The howling wind turned into a shriek, the sound of a mother losing her child. The trailer rocked heavily. The lights went out and the windows blew, covering us both with glass. Bobby tumbled off the sofa towards me.

"She's on Her way. Stay calm," he hollered. But he sounded worried. I saw fear on his face.

"Take my hand."

"No, you hold on to me."

Then everything went quiet and dark. Cave dark. There was a sucking sound. My ears popped.

"I smell it," he cried. "Roses."

He was mistaken, of course. It wasn't roses. I screamed, "Sulphur," and saw his confusion. He reached for me, but too late. I was gone.

\*

I landed in a field, without a scratch. I don't remember much. A lifting sensation, whirling, not so much falling as floating and landing gently, as if set down by a hand. I remember the colour of the sky – soft dusky pink. Like the flowers we had at the house.

We found Bobby in a tree. In shock, bruised to hell and babbling. The church roof was torn off, the steeple in a ditch. They'd be repaired with time and money. There was no sign of the trailer anywhere. Ever. Nothing in town was damaged. Trees were blown over, but the main damage occurred outside town.

Bobby spent three weeks in hospital. He was unconscious the first time I came. The second too. But the doctors were sure he'd come out of it. He had a stream of visitors praying for him, so I left them to it. The third week I found him on his own and awake. He saw me and grinned.

"Only took Mary three days to check on Jesus."

"Bobby—"

He didn't let me finish.

"Grace, I'm sorry. For everything. You were right."

I hadn't expected that, but I wanted to be sure what he was saying.

"About what?" I asked, wondering if he understood his answer would decide our future.

He took my hand. "I know the sacrifices you've made. And I shouldn't have left the family. But in some ways, we were both right..."

I sighed, shook my head, pulled my hand back. He held it tight. I couldn't move away.

"You were... more right... Grace... it's just that... when I looked up at the sky... I wanted to see something special too."

I forgave him then. It's what Jesus would do. But I didn't let him off the hook. Got him a radio for his tractor cab which he keeps turned up loud. Got him an air freshener too. Royal Pine scent. We hired more hands to help out. And started evening classes. Bobby's taking Star Gazing for Beginners. I'm doing a refresher in Physics. Then maybe I'll look into teaching.

We still compromise on things. That's how marriage works. But they're compromises we can live with. When Bobby brought home a toaster that imprints the image of Our Blessed Mother on bread, I let it slide. In fact, I use it sometimes on the sandwiches I pack for him. Gives him a little thrill while he's out in the fields. He comes back at the end of the day asking if I know of any angels needing a good ravishing. Overall, we're back on track. I even called up Rae last week. Asked if February was a good time to visit.

"Perfect," she said. "Not too hot and good viewing conditions."

"Excellent," I replied. "That's what we want. Clear skies."

I spread jam over my toast, covering Mary's face, and considered myself blessed.

~

## Sherry Morris's Biography

Originally from Missouri, America's heartland, Sherry writes monologues, short stories and flash fiction which have won prizes, been placed on shortlists and performed in London and Scotland.

After 17 years in London working as a university administrator, Sherry moved to a farm in the Scottish Highlands where she goes for long walks, watches clouds and dreams up stories. Her first publication appeared in *A Small Key Opens Big Doors* and reflects on her Peace Corps experience in Ukraine during the early 1990's.

Her published stories can be found on www.uksherka.com or follow her on Twitter: @Uksherka

# MY GIRLFRIEND'S HANDBAG

*Shortlisted story, by Gina Parsons*

I met her at Dan's barbecue. I assumed he knew her or that she was a friend of a friend. But it turned out no one knew her at all. They all said they 'vaguely remembered someone' from my description of her – flawless olive skin, long dark hair, slightly taller than your average woman (but not in a circus freak kind of a way), and eyes that changed colour depending on her mood – but no one could say for certain. It was as if she had been shrouded in some kind of perception filter making her unnoticeable to everyone except me.

She was sitting alone under the gazebo, cradling a glass of wine.

"That's quite a small handbag you've got there," I said, tilting my half empty pint glass towards it.

She ran her fingers along its gold satin fringe.

"There can't be much more in there than, say, purse? Keys? Phone?"

"Sure," she shrugged, sipped her wine, avoided eye-contact.

"Here." I stretched my arm out towards the little black bag. "Let me see."

"No." She snatched it up and slung it under her armpit.

"Come on, let me see if I'm right."

"No there's... things in there."

The hairs on the back of my neck stood up. "What things?"

"Precious things."

"Like what?"

"Oh, you know," she waved her hand dismissively and leaned back in her chair. "Women's things."

"Like Tampax and stuff?"

"What?"

"In your bag. Tampax and stuff. It's hardly precious though, is it? I mean, precious is more like, I don't know, jewellery, photos, personal possessions, you know?" I scrutinized her as I gulped down the last of my beer. "Besides," I persisted, convinced she was about to give in. "It can't be any worse than the kind of stuff my mum carried around in hers."

She glared at me, her eyes darkened. "You went in your mum's handbag?"

Dad would always say it was a no-go area. Then he'd laugh and say, "Don't go in there, son. You might not come back out." If he needed anything out of it, like the car keys or whatever, he'd ask Mum to get them. It was always closed, never more than a few inches from her side, and whenever I went to touch it she'd smack my hand away. It went everywhere with her. In the car, to the bathroom, in bed. And when she died, it disappeared.

"Yeah," I lied. "It fell over once, and some stuff fell out."

"And you saw it all?"

"Yeah. It's no big deal..." I hoped she wouldn't call my bluff. I never went in Mum's handbag.

"Well," she snapped. "That wouldn't happen now. They're much more... robust these days. Less likely to, you know, just pop open like that."

At this point I hoped she'd open it. But she didn't. She eased into a smile and gave her bag a reassuring stroke. I was smitten.

*

A few weeks later, I lounged on the bed while she showered. Her handbag was bigger this time, with a large gold magnetic clasp at the centre, and she'd left it resting up against the headboard. I tried not to look at it, but it silently urged me on: *open me, open me*. The more I tried to ignore it, the more my hands twitched until I found myself leaning across the bed and stretching my arm out towards it. My fingertips brushed against the clasp just as she unlocked the bathroom door. I catapulted the bag off the bed and grabbed the remote control.

"What was that?" She stood in the doorway, wearing my dressing gown, red-faced from the shower.

"What was what?"

"That loud thump."

"I didn't hear anything." I scrolled through Netflix, my thumb jabbing the button faster and faster. "Good shower?"

She didn't answer. She stomped around the bed and glared at me. "Did you do this?" She pointed at the bag on the floor.

"N-no," I said.

"How did it end up down there then?"

I shrugged. "I dunno."

"Don't you ever, ever, touch my bag again," she yelled, almost foaming at the mouth. She picked up the bag, held it in her arms and stroked it.

She settled the bag on the nightstand beside her. We lay there in the dark that night, back-to-back, barely touching.

*

She came round to my flat often and each time carrying a different bag, a bigger one, a blacker one, and she went everywhere with it. In bed, it'd take up its position beside her, its clasps, buckles and zips gleaming in the light from the overhead lamp. I'd loiter around it, but she'd always move it away and when she went in it for something, my god, she went in elbow deep. One time, she went in so far, her head almost disappeared.

I did that once. Mum kept her tattered old handbags in a dusty brown suitcase under her bed and whenever she'd yell at me to, "For God's sake, go and play," that's where I'd go. I'd rummage around, relishing the thrill of opening and closing her discarded handbags. There was never anything in them, but I liked to squeeze one of my arms inside to feel the lining against my skin. I'd close my eyes and imagine being small enough to fit inside. Maybe then, I reckoned, I could be the thing Mum carried everywhere with her. I could be the thing she could never let out of her sight. I could be the most important thing she needed to keep close.

Once, just once, I was so desperate I pushed my head through the opening and breathed in the scent of old copper coins and Murray Mints. It was fucking amazing. I caught my ears and hair on the open zip as I pulled back though. It hurt like hell, but I wanted to do it again. I wanted to see how far I could go.

*

One night, we were curled up on the sofa watching a film when she went to the loo and left her bag behind. She never did that and maybe it was a test, I don't know, but I couldn't resist. As soon as I heard her close the bathroom door, I grabbed at it from beside the sofa. I pulled so hard on the zip that it left indent marks on my fingers but no matter how hard I yanked and wrestled with it, it wouldn't budge. I threw it down and kicked it back into place just as she walked through the door.

"All right?" she said.

"Yeah," I said, sucking my red swollen fingers.

I thought I could handle it, but I couldn't. I was going to break up with her.

Of course, I made the mistake of waiting for the right time to tell her. But when the whole, "I'm pregnant," thing happened, and she came back from the clinic with a black chenille carpet bag the size of a suitcase, I freaked out. It was huge and had multiple zips, brass buckles and clasps, and buttoned down outer pockets threaded with gold silk. I couldn't break up with her now.

*

"I'm just nipping out to the pub," I said, and handed her a cup of tea.

"Now?"

"Yeah." I sat in the armchair and pulled on my trainers. I couldn't get them on quick enough. "I said I'd meet the lads for a quick one or two."

"It's a bit late, isn't it?"

I looked at my watch. "It's only eight."

"Well, what time will you be back?"

"God, I don't know, 10? 11-ish?"

She slammed the mug down on the coffee table, folded her arms and stared at the TV. "Right. Fine."

"Oh, come on," I said. "Don't be like that."

"No, it's fine, fine. You go out. Have a wonderful time."

I bent down to kiss her but stubbed my toe on her bag tucked down by the side of the sofa. "For fuck's sake," I shouted. My big toe throbbed. "Your fucking bag..."

"Don't," she hissed. "Go on, get out."

I slammed the front door behind me so hard it sprung back open. "Fuck it."

*

It was gone 12 when I crashed out of the pub doors and

by the time I got home it was so dark I could barely see the stone doorstep, let alone the door itself. I used my fingertips to guide the key into the lock and stumbled into the hallway. I wasn't paralytic, just drunk enough to take the edge off, but the fifth pint hadn't helped my negotiation of the dark.

"For fuck's sake," I yelled. "You could've left me a fucking light on." I didn't care if she was asleep. I wanted her awake.

I staggered down the hallway and kicked open the bedroom door. The bedside lamp was on and she was sitting up in bed with her arms folded.

"You're awake then." I fell forwards on to the bed. "Good."

"Hard not to be," she said.

"We..." I rolled on to my back and tried to pull off my trainers, "need to talk."

"What about?"

I launched one trainer through the open doorway and fumbled with my shirt buttons. "I've had enough."

"Yeah, it sounds like it. What did you have, four pints? Five pints? Ten?"

I rolled over on to my front again. "You," I snarled at her. "I've had enough of you." I wanted to rile her but the calmer she was the more irritated I became. "You." I pointed my finger right in her face. "You and your fucking handbag."

She smoothed the duvet across her lap and sighed. "Not this again." She looked away from me towards the bag. "Look," she said. "I could show you but..."

"I don't bloody care, sweetheart, I—" I rolled over, misjudged the edge of the bed, and fell off, hitting my head on the corner of the bedside table. On my knees, I lay my head on the corner of the bed and as my eyes began to close, succumbing to the pain and the need for sleep, I heard a loud *CLICK*.

"My mother never said she loved me, you know?" she said. "She never said it, but I could tell she did. I could see it in her eyes."

"Uh-huh." I didn't move, didn't care.

"Do you want to see?"

"No. Sod off." I kept my eyes closed.

"Look," she said. "Just look." I opened one eye and saw in her hands a pale blue glasses case.

I groped at the duvet and hauled myself up on to the bed. She slowly opened the case and smiled. "I've got my mother's eyes," she whispered and turned the case towards me.

I took it from her and stared at the contents. They looked like two white cue balls on a sheet of crumpled blue baize. Only, with eyelids. And eyelashes. And beautiful blue irises with deep black pupils. I dropped it and leapt up off the bed. "What the fuck?" I said, wiping my hands down the sides of my jeans. "What the..."

"Now, my father," she said, "he was a real bastard." She put both her hands inside the bag up to her wrists. "But, I know he loved me... in his heart." She tugged it free from inside the bag with both hands and, as it slid on to the duvet, it pulsated. It was a heart. An actual fucking heart. With a pulse. And thick blue veins. And a brownish tinge on one side and it smelled bad, like a rotting carcass.

I leaned back against the chest of drawers to steady myself. Without saying a word, she reached back into the bag, this time up to her elbows.

"No." I put my hand out. "Don't tell me... the next thing out is your sister's fucking head or something." I bent double, gripped my knees, and retched.

She paused, resting her elbows on the outer edge of the bag letting her hands dangle inside. "Oh, I don't have a sister," she said mournfully.

I peered up at her.

"I had a brother once though..."

"Jesus fuck..." My knees began to give way.

"Don't worry. I didn't keep anything of his. He was a bit, you know, unstable."

"Unstable? He was unstable?"

"Yeah, I don't really want to talk about it."

I kicked out at the foot of the bed. The bag toppled over, the inside of it faced me. There were rows and rows of little compartments, buttoned-down pouches, large and small zippered sections, and satin pockets.

She turned and picked fluff off her sleeve before reaching forward to pull the bag upright. A small bundle wrapped in tissue paper rolled out.

"What the fuck is that?"

"Oh, it's nothing," she said, stuffing the small bundle back into the bag. "I'm really tired now so..."

"It's not nothing. Show me." It was shaped like a Russian doll and, underneath the tissue, where the paper had torn, it looked like pink blancmange with little bits of fine white downy hair.

"Can we finish this another time?" she said.

"No, we're doing it now." I grasped anything I could and threw them at her; deodorant cans, a hairbrush, the remote control. I pulled out my sock drawer, ready to throw the whole thing at her when she put her hands up and screamed, "OK, OK. All right, all right."

"Well?" I said, the drawer falling beside me, socks spilling out across the bedroom floor.

"It's the one thing you didn't want," she said. "A baby. Our baby."

I fell to my knees, puked on the carpet, and passed out.

*

I came to and she was standing over me, pulling me up by my wrists.

"What's that noise?" I said, my mouth and tongue so dry I could just about get the words out.

"Oh, it's nothing," she said. "If you could just stand…"

She didn't let go of me as I struggled to my feet. She pinned me against the bed with her legs. Behind me, her bag lay trembling, groaning, and dribbling against the pillows.

"What's it doing?" I slurred.

"Don't worry," she said. "It's adjusting itself."

I could feel myself drifting again. "Adjusting itself?"

"Yes," she said. "For you."

*

I came to as she grappled with my head, forcing it inside the bag.

*

I came to, on the floor, my head slick with phlegm, and she sat crying, cradling the bag, rocking to and fro. "I'm sorry," she cried. "I'm so sorry."

*

I came to, damp with sweat, spread-eagled on the bed.

The bag nestled beside me, its tattered body silent and still. I reached out my hand, pulled it in towards me, and stroked it. I caught a whiff of old copper coins and Murray Mints as its mouth gently closed. Exhausted, we lay together in the dark.

~

## Gina Parsons' Biography

Gina Parsons is a writer based in Brighton where she lives with her family. She has a PGCert with Distinction in Creative Writing from the University of Chichester and is currently fine-tuning a range of short stories while avoiding the shitty first draft of her novel.

You can find her on Twitter: @LittleBookishHQ

# SHADOW LEGS

## *Shortlisted story, by Michele Sheldon*

Gracie often admired her shadow self on sunny days, marvelling at how impossibly long and thin her legs were. Almost the length of a giraffe's, she'd think to herself.

She liked to imagine what it would feel like to own them, to parade up and down Sunny Sands on those fine pins. To feel the warmth of admiring glances and the coldness of envious stares. She visualised just how they'd feel to walk on; light and delicate but strong and flexible.

So, when her shadow sidles up to her one day, and asks if she'd like to do a leg swap, how could she resist?

*

She hits the High Street straight away. Visits every clothes shop. Tries on all the skinny jeans she can find. Whoops in delight as she squeezes her shadow legs into a size eight in every store, five sizes smaller than normal. And best of all, she doesn't have to roll up a single pair. She even has to complain in one shop because the jeans stop short of her ankles. But she can live with not being able to shop there. With her legs 11, she realises she's going to have to rethink her usual retail habits. Her and her skinny legs have so outgrown the local shopping centre and she promises herself a visit to a more upmarket mall, Westfield perhaps, to match her new glamorous self. She skips towards home, only too aware of the gawps of fellow shoppers, many of whom, she is delighted to see, include several girls from the year above.

It's Saturday tomorrow, she realises with relish. She's already arranged to meet her best friend, Freya, at Sunny Sands and can't wait. Never again would she have to hide under her towel to take her clothes off, or sit near the shoreline so she could run straight into the sea as soon as she undressed. She'd pose next to the arches. Even better the steps, where everyone worth knowing gathered. She'd hang around at the top, sniggering at the sunbathers toasting their doughy flesh as they wallowed like pigs among their discarded lager cans, plastic bags and Poundland snacks. Then, she'd saunter down to the sea, where she'd make a great display of kicking at the waves. She felt like she may spontaneously start dancing, but decided that may be a bit over the top, a bit like showing off. She'd have to try and be a bit humble about her great legs, especially as they were now longer and thinner than Freya.

No one had longer or thinner legs than Freya's.

To be honest, she wasn't sure how Freya would take it. You see, there was an unwritten rule between them whereby Gracie had the best nose and mouth and Freya, the best legs. It was a delicate balance of power, dictated by playground peers since primary school.

But now the nose/mouth versus legs power axis had shifted, she didn't know whether Freya would still want to be friends with her.

In fact, did she even want to be friends with Freya? Did she even need Freya, she wonders as she spots Charisma and Channel coming up the Old High Street, tucking into a bag of chips.

"Wow, you look amazing," says Charisma.

"Almost like you've been super-stretched," says Channel, staring at her legs.

Gracie blushes under their gaze, unsure how to deal with this new found attention from the most popular girls at school.

"I mean is it like… like… one of those new celebrity treatments? The stretching rack?" she asks.

An image from a documentary of common medieval tortures pops into Gracie's head. "No."

"Big Bang then?" asks Channel.

For a split second Gracie is completely thrown. She wonders if Channel wants her to say something meaningful about the beginning of the universe. What with Stephen Hawking dying so recently, was theoretical physics the new thing to be in to?

"The Big Bang. The new celeb diet?" she explains.

Of course, thinks Gracie. Charisma and Channel are always on a diet, even when they're consuming chips, fizzy drinks, crisps and chocolate.

Gracie wonders whether to come clean and tell them the truth. But then everyone will have long, skinny legs and she's wanted them for so long. It didn't seem fair that everyone else should have a pair.

"You know? Eat nothing bigger than an at-om," says Charisma.

"My aunt tried it and had to be hospitalised after a week," adds Channel.

"5-2 diet?" asks Charisma, looking her up and down.

Gracie nods, vaguely recognising the diet as one of many she's read about.

"It's worked wonders for you," says Channel, a chip poised in her hand as she stares at Gracie's legs and shakes her head in awe.

"We're going to the beach tomorrow if you want to come?" says Charisma.

"I'm meeting Freya."

The two look at each other and roll their eyes.

"Low tide at midday. We'll be in the fourth arch along and whatever you do… don't bring Freya," says Channel.

*

Gracie's mum gives her a double-take as she leaves the house.

"You've grown again. In a day?"

"I haven't seen you for three days, Mum."

"Still. You'll be through the roof before long."

Gracie wonders if she should tell her the truth. Find

out if it's OK to swap body parts with your shadow, but her mum's already half way out of the door.

"Tea's in the oven. Dad'll be home at nine. If you need anything, go next door. And no more growing. Love you," she calls as she slams the door in Gracie's face.

Gracie stares at the door's peeling blue paint, trying to recall if she's ever overheard her parents, or any friends talking about shadows asking to swap. She didn't remember seeing any 'shadow stranger danger' public health warning films. She certainly didn't learn about it in biology. It's got to be safe, she reasons.

But just in case, she Googles it. She scans down pages and pages of articles written by male fitness gurus screaming 'From fat to fit in 9 days' and 'How you can REALLY change your body in 79 easy steps' and there's even one about 'Getting rid of women's ugly strawberry legs'. Gracie's mouth hangs open. The day was indeed turning very strange. It's on a par, she thinks, with the day she came across a video about the Milkmen, a whole movement of men breast feeding babies. Of course, she'd never heard of 'ugly strawberry legs', let alone that women worldwide are inflicted by the condition. As she imagines her torso attached to two giant juicy strawberries, her leg swapping issues begin to pale into insignificance. Thoughts crash around Gracie's head, vying for attention. How would you stop strawberry lovers taking a bite out of your legs? Or did the ugly strawberry reference refer to yet another shape to shame women with? Eventually her mind calms as she reads on; it's a reference to little pin pricks of red that show up after shaving your legs. Gracie looks down at her shadow legs and smiles. They're as smooth and hairless as the Hollywood.

She fetches her tea from the fridge and, crunching on a lettuce leaf, decides there must be no other explanation than she made it happen, just like all those positive thinking quotes littering social media. You could literally think yourself a new pair of legs. There wasn't a day she hadn't bemoaned the uncomfortable feeling of fat rubbing between the top of her thighs, the cellulite that'd seemingly appeared overnight, the mean remarks from boys during games about her being a Russian weightlifter. Every time she inadvertently caught a glimpse of her legs in the mirror, she'd felt a little piece of herself shrivel inside. They didn't belong to her. They didn't fit with the rest of her slim, boyish figure.

And now she'd got what she wanted, should she share this new found knowledge with the world? Become a YouTuber, amassing millions of hits, not to mention a fortune? Apply it to other areas of her life? Grade 9s in her GSCEs? Lottery win for Mum and Dad? World peace?

*

Nightmares plague Gracie that night. She dreams she wakes in the morning to find nothing but her crinkled sheet where her legs should be. Only when she pulls herself across the bed to the window and opens her curtains, the sunlight flooding into her bedroom, do her new legs reappear. She spends all morning checking in every single mirror that her legs remain attached to her body. And when she steps out into the sunshine, she breathes a big sigh of relief; her usual shadow is waiting for her, lolling across the driveway.

Gracie walks to the steps leading to Sunny Sands,

trying to ignore the dozens of messages from Freya, as well as the odd sensation of lightness in her legs. She turns off her phone and distracts herself from the floaty feeling by looking across to the beach below. Hundreds of people have already marked out their territory, and are busy building elaborate sandcastles, sunbathing or splashing about in the gentle waves. Families weighted down with huge beach bags, overflowing with towels, buckets and spades, pass by on their way home for lunch. She feels something twist inside her as she fondly remembers doing the same, not so long ago, when life was so much simpler and she wasn't expected to be anything but a child.

She climbs down the steps, aware of how her cotton trousers no longer flap around her legs but almost invade them. How stupidly weightless her legs feel as if they may dissolve at any moment. They're certainly not the lithe, supple limbs she'd imagined and is pleased she wore trainers and not flip-flops, and relieved there's only a gentle sea breeze, otherwise her legs were in danger of floating off across the Channel or the White Cliffs. And there's something else troubling Gracie. She can see now that her shadow legs cast a much lighter shadow compared to her body. Like someone got fed up with shading in her legs and went off to do something more interesting. And she wonders for the first time when she can get her real legs back.

"Bagged the best spot," says Channel when Gracie arrives.

"And if I put the music on, and have a smoke, then that lot will disappear," Charisma says, pointing to several groups of families sitting directly in front of them.

Gracie holds her bag to her chest as if the very act

will make her feel more grounded. She tries to think of an excuse to leave. She'll call Freya. Tell her everything.

But Charisma grabs her bag and dumps it into the gloomy arch.

"Come on then," says Channel, stripping off to her sparkly orange bikini. "We've been waiting so we could all go in together. Give the lard-arses something to aspire to."

Gracie pulls down her leggings, pleased to be distracted by someone doing acrobatics along the shoreline, near the rock pools. Whoever it is, they've drawn quite a crowd of small children with their cart wheeling and flipping in and out of the waves. There's something mesmerising about the fluid movement of the legs, the sheer energy of the display and even the legs themselves. They're muscular and athletic and strangely familiar. She squints into the sun to get a better look, thinking perhaps it's someone from her gymnastics class from a couple of years ago. But they're spinning through the waves so quickly they look like a cartoon blur, almost like they don't have a body. And as they slow and resurface from the sea, she realises the legs aren't actually attached to a body because they're her legs. Though far more slender than she remembers.

"Where…? What…?" says Channel, who is now backing away from her, pointing at her legs for all the wrong reasons.

When Gracie glances down, she sees her torso is hanging over her beach towel and feels herself sinking.

She looks up to see her magnificent legs are hurtling towards her, coming back to her at last; somersaulting through the gaps between sunbathers, kicking sand into faces and over picnics. A little blond toddler starts squealing in delight. His mother sweeps him up in her arms as the legs whirl by. Other people are screaming, scrambling to their feet and fleeing up the steps or into the water, leaving their belongings scattered over the beach. And Gracie feels nauseous as she remembers something she'd forgotten from her dream; the sensation of being tricked by her shadow.

She musters all her strength and drags herself along the sand, away from the darkness of the archway into the sunlight, her shadow legs reappearing. Hover-sprinting, she catches up with her legs near to the rock pools and tackles them to the ground, trying several times to sit atop them and force them back into position. But they're too slippery with sun lotion and sweat, and far too powerful. They wriggle free from beneath her and leap into the sea, vanishing as her shadow head emerges through a wave, laughing.

"You can't catch me."

~

## Michele Sheldon's Biography

Michele's short stories have been published in a diverse range of anthologies including *Stories for Homes*, and magazines including *Rosebud, Storgy* and *Here Comes Everyone*.

# THE CHEAT

*Shortlisted story, by Karen Jones*

Peter's hospital chart read: Jostled by herd (shoal? I dunno – this is a first) of angry seahorses. No obvious injury. Just a bit weird. Overnight observation.

Peter tried to tell the doctor there was nothing weird here. For the past nine months he'd attracted misfortune, mayhem and potentially life-threatening injury the way some people attract static, though if Peter got a shock from an elevator button it would most likely be the result of a freak accident re-routing 4,000 volts through it. But he would survive. That was the thing about Peter; he always survived.

Discovering his affinity with the indestructible Captain Scarlet had come as a relief. He faced each new day a stoic: it would be bad, it would hurt, but he would live. His misfortunes had the opposite effect on his wife, whose stoicism disappeared as quickly as vodka at a hen party. Visiting him in hospital after his encounter with the seemingly satanic seahorses, she explained her position as gently as she could.

"I can't take it anymore. It's like living with a cartoon. Wile E Coyote has less bizarre accidents than you. And you just keep smiling that inane, goofy – Jesus, I can't get cartoons out my head – that stupid smile. Why don't you get angry? Why don't you get a priest to exorcise you? Why don't you do *something*, for fuck's sake?"

He winced when she swore – he hated coarseness in women. She hadn't always been that way. She had been a sweet little thing when he married her. He couldn't think what had caused the change in her personality.

He shrugged, ran his fingers through his ever-tumbling blond hair and gave her one of his sweetest smiles. "What can I do? I'm anointed."

She grabbed a handful of hospital blanket and squeezed it until her knuckles went white. "Anointed? You're cursed – why can't you see it?"

He patted her clawed hand. "I'm alive. How many people could go through what I have and live? Someone's looking out for me."

"Someone with a rubber mallet, a 10-tonne anvil and a grand piano on a shaky pulley is looking out for you. I can't live like this. I need to get up in the morning and know that, for just one day, I won't have to visit a hospital or the police station or the Ministry of Defence. I'm sorry, Peter, I do love you, but from now on, you're on your own."

As he watched her walk out of the room, his future looked less certain. Not only would he have to face endless rounds of being stuck in lifts, revolving doors and chest freezers – not only would he suffer the ignominy of being attacked by a variety of normally benign life forms, from household pets to sheep and sea urchins – now he would have to face it alone. He did, for one moment, consider calling her back and repeating his 'what can I do?' face and case to her, but something stopped him.

That something was the sound of his wife screaming as she stumbled over a sharps bucket that had been dropped by a hospital porter who had tripped over the nurse who was bending down to un-snag her tights from the nail that, somehow, was sticking out of Peter's hospital room door. The last words Peter heard from his wife were screamed. "Bastard, your condition is contagious."

He knew he'd miss her, even miss the expletives, but he remained so sure of his status as a 'lucky man', he assumed she'd come back to him.

In the six weeks following her departure, Peter's life continued to meander along its stream of bizarre incidents: Stung by a previously unclassified species of bee, to which he developed an allergic reaction; chased by an escaped ostrich – no one ever established from where it had made its bid for freedom – and run over by a Smart Car unleashed by a seven-year-old child who claimed he thought it was a giant's roller skate.

Apart from a little ointment for the bee sting and a couple of his usual overnight-for-observation stays in

A&E, he needed no treatment and became convinced this proved his theory: Not only was he anointed and indestructible, his body had become so inured to the constant onslaught of unlikely accidents it no longer manifested the physical results of the punishment it took. His conviction that 'someone' was looking out for him changed his smile from 'goofy' to positively beatific.

The day the letter arrived, Peter got out of bed, stretched, yawned, fell over his own shoes and hit his head on the bedside table, rendering himself unconscious for two minutes. When he came around he smiled. Another day, another disaster – there was something to be said for consistency.

He ambled to the front door to retrieve the mail, opened the lawyer's letter, then slid down the wall, his eyes darting from line to line in the document detailing the divorce petition. Unreasonable behaviour? Irreconcilable differences? Could she really be going through with it? He thought she'd miss him, realise that his 'condition' was a blessing – he would never die in an accident, only disease would take him from her, and even that seemed increasingly unlikely.

Peter's previously permanent smile vanished. He had coped admirably without her for six weeks but forever looked like a different and frightening prospect. Life without her seemed impossible. Worse – life without her seemed pointless.

He allowed his mind to wander to dark and dangerous territory. What if his theory was wrong? What if he only survived because he believed he would? If he stopped believing, would one of the accidents prove fatal? What if he actively tried to die?

He dragged himself up off the floor and went into the kitchen where he switched on the toaster then, as carefully and calmly as he could, held a knife in one of the slots. The electricity surged through his body, intense pain crackled along his nerves – then it stopped. Everything stopped. The electric clock, the microwave, the ceiling fan, the radio – all dead. Peter, on the other hand, was resolutely alive.

He took out the sharpest, sturdiest knife he could find, opened the dishwasher, put the knife in the cutlery basket sharp end up, then threw himself on top of it. It bent. He stood up and inspected his chest to find nothing more than the beginnings of a mild bruise. The dishwasher door hadn't fared so well and was hanging off its hinges.

Peter did something he hadn't done in a long time. He took a deep breath and screamed. The noise echoed around the house, serving only as a reminder of his solitude. The bent knife, mangled toaster and wrecked dishwasher a searing indictment of his ineptitude. He couldn't die even if he wanted to – where was the justice in that?

That was when he heard the voice. At first he thought he had left the radio on, but then remembered the power cut. Next he considered madness. It would hardly be surprising under the circumstances. He closed his eyes and concentrated on not hearing the voice.

"Don't be so bloody stupid. Now you know I'm here there's no getting rid of me, mate."

The voice sounded close to his ear, but there was no one else in the room. He searched everywhere until he felt a gentle tug at his ear lobe. He looked down at his shoulder to find a tiny, grubby, smelly little man smiling at him – a disturbingly black-toothed smile accompanied by a stench from his breath that belied his size.

"What the hell...?"

The man rolled his eyes. "Don't give me any of that crap – you know perfectly well who I am. You've been telling everyone who would listen. 'Ooo, look at me, I'm anointed, I am. There's someone looking out for me. I'm so lucky.' So don't start pretending you're shocked. Shocked... like you were a minute ago, eh?" The little man was very pleased with his joke and rolled around on Peter's shoulder, laughing his foul socks off.

Peter frowned. "You're my Guardian Angel?"

"Ah, now there's a lot of confusion about that sort of thing. You can't just go bandying the words Guardian Angel around. Not that they don't exist – they do. They're a bit arsey, truth be told. Right up themselves. Thing is, every sad-act that gets saved claims to have one. But that's not what I am."

Peter waited, but no further explanation was forthcoming. "Well, what are you then?"

The creature folded his arms and stuck out his jaw. "I'm an irritant. I'm a foil. I'm a right pain in the arse – and a compulsive gambler, which is where you come in. I'm the only thing that gets right up Death's nose."

"Death?" Peter allowed himself a sceptical smile. "You mean black cloak, scythe, egg-timer Death?"

The man pulled himself up to his full height of about three inches. "No, I mean all around you, in your face, doesn't like having the piss taken out of him Death, so watch your lip. He gets bored, see, so he has a few of us going around trying to save people that he tries to kill. You're my best project yet – you've lasted longer than any mark I've ever had. If I can keep you alive for another three months I get to come back to life – full size and everything."

"You mean you're human?"

"Of course I'm human, you cheeky sod. They have to shrink us when we die or we wouldn't all fit. How stupid are you? We do get special, um, well, power-type things to allow us to save idiots, though."

Peter realised he was suffering from delusions, probably brought on by concussion from his early morning fall. He smiled at the little man. "OK, well I'm going to go and lie down now. It was lovely to meet you and I'm sorry you won't be here when I wake up, because I've really quite enjoyed your company – ow."

The little man's teeth sunk into Peter's ear. "Feel that, did you? I'm real, OK? Now, you listen to me. I want to win this bet. I can't have you making it more difficult. Trying to kill yourself, helping Death, that's no way to behave."

"But my wife…"

"Yeah, yeah, I know all about it – big deal. Just give me three months. If I keep you alive for that length of time, Death has to back off – that's part of the deal. The accidents will stop. When that happens, she'll come back to you, won't she?"

Peter thought about it. He supposed it was worth a try.

"OK. I think. Yes. Why not? And what does Death get if he…?"

The spear that sailed through the open window and lodged itself snugly in his chest cut Peter's words short. He hit the floor, the little voice in his ear screaming at someone he couldn't see. "You dirty cheating bastard. I took my eye off the ball for a moment, I'll give you that, but a spear? A fucking spear?"

As Peter slipped into his final bout of unconsciousness he heard a hollow laugh and a surprisingly high-pitched voice address the little man.

"You said any reasonable weapon. There's a war society re-enacting a battle in the field across the road. It seemed like fair game. You lose. Now, where's my Space Hopper?"

Peter's life for a Space Hopper – it seemed oddly appropriate.

~

## Karen Jones's Biography

Karen Jones is a prose writer from Glasgow with a preference for flash and short fiction. She has been successful in various writing competitions including Mslexia, Flash 500, Words With Jam, New Writer, Writers' Forum, Writers' Bureau and Ad Hoc Fiction.

Her work has appeared in numerous magazines and ezines, most recently in *Nottingham Review, Lost Balloon* and *Reflex Fiction*. Stories have been printed in anthologies including *Bath Short Story Award, To Hull And Back, The Wonderful World of Worders* and *Bath Flash Fiction*.

In 2014 she published a short story collection, *The Upside-Down Jesus and other stories*. She recently judged The Federation of Writers (Scotland) Flash Fiction Competition and was a reader for TSS Publishing.

# THE CURSE OF THE GIGANTIC FINGER

*Shortlisted story, by Rachel McHale*

This all happened the day I cut off the tip of my right index finger on a televised cooking competition, which is actually a much less interesting story than you might imagine. The only noteworthy bit was when the nurse put the dressing on. She had a cool gadget to help her twiddle the gauze around to ensure effective coverage of my finger. I admired the nurse's handiwork in the taxi home.

I yelped when I stubbed my finger on the door handle. The thing about the bandage was that it was gigantic. I looked like I was wearing one of those huge sponge hands that Yanks wear to baseball games. My roommate, Nigel, said the words I would come to dread. "What happened to your hand?"

I told him the story. "You cut the tip of your finger off on TV?" He could barely stand he was laughing so much.

"Not live TV – it'll be on air next week."

"What night?" he asked. "I am SO having everyone round. We can serve finger foods."

In that moment, I really wished the gigantic bandage was on my middle finger. "Yeah, yeah. Hilarious."

"You're going to be a total babe magnet after that, aren't you?"

I thought about Matt's housewarming party next Friday. I pictured chatting up some wavy-haired goddess who resembled Nigella and wouldn't take the piss out of me for watching the *Bake Off*. It would be great, until my mates decided to play my clip from YouTube.

"Fuck off, Nige," I said. Then, "Fuck." I was having a fight with a can of beer.

"Aww, mate, does PeeteyWeetey need a wittle hewp wiv his dwink?" said Nigel.

I punched his shoulder, then dropped the can as I reeled and clutched my hand. "Fuck, fuck, fuck."

I think my eyes may have even filled with tears, because he said, "That's it. You're coming out with me."

I noticed Nigel was wearing his best suit and a garish, patterned red tie that belonged at a haematology convention.

"Didn't you say you had an important meeting tonight with some clients? I believe your words were 'life or death'. I'm not sure I should gate-crash that.

Much as I could do with a drink someone else poured for me."

"Er, the thing is, mate," Nigel's eyes bounced around the room. "I lied."

"OK," I said slowly.

"I don't have a meeting, per se. I'm, erm, going, um, speed dating."

"You're shitting me. *Speed dating?*"

"Yeah, well, I'm planning on meeting a dozen women tonight, what are your plans?"

TV. Takeaway. Beer if I can get one open. Pity party. "Fair point," I said.

"You should come along."

"I dunno, mate, speed dating. Sounds pretty lame."

"After that show airs next week, you'll be lucky to have a conversation that doesn't involve some girl laughing her pants off – and not in a good way. Think of it as a last chance saloon before you're exiled to dating Siberia."

\*

So, here I am, ready to meet my first 'date'. When I see her, I smile up at the gods. She has cinnamon hair, neat little ears, and a curvy figure that my hands are itching to skim. She's hot. Let's elope to Gibraltar hot.

She gives me a smile that would mesmerise me, if I didn't have such a good view down her shirt. "Hi, I'm Pete," I say, extending my hand. And there's my bandage, glowing white in the dim light. I pull it back.

"Carly," she replies. "What happened to your hand?"

"It's not a very interesting story. I'd rather hear about you."

"I broke my finger once," she says.

"Really?" I ask, trying to find a way off the subject. "And what do you do for a living?"

"Yeah, this horrible boy at school pushed me over. There was an actual crack, I'm telling you."

"I'd never do that, push a girl over, I mean. He sounds awful. Where did you go to school? Did you grow up in Manchester?"

"Oh, he grew up OK. He's my ex-husband, as a matter of fact."

"Oh, right. So..."

"Don't worry, we're divorced now. But my finger's never been quite the same." She holds out her hand and shows me her slightly crooked index finger. "I mean, it's still good for pointing and such." She demonstrates. "But I'll never be a hand model."

I look at her hands, delicate with tiny purple veins. I start to worry about all the things I'm not going to be able to do with my finger. Honestly, by the time the bell rings, I'm relieved.

\*

I avoid holding out my hand to the next date, carefully putting it in my lap instead. I look at her and blink, several times. She sparkles. Not in an I'm-instantly-love-struck kind of way, but in a wow-that's-a-lot-of-shiny-things kind of way. I'm tempted to use my gigantic finger as a sun visor.

"Lila, I presume," I say, gesturing to the sequinned letters spackled over the front of her jacket.

"It's fab, isn't it? I made it myself. Well, not the jacket, but I decorated it."

And she's away, talking about the nitty gritty of bedecking, showing me her huge glittering handbag and her blinged up T-shirt. My crazy alarm is ringing but if you can get underneath the glare of the plastic gems and tinsel (yes, her T-shirt actually has tinsel on it) she's quite attractive, so I try to focus on imagining her without the clothes. But all I can picture is a bedroom with a gem-studded lampshade and teddy bears dressed for a disco.

I pick up my pint as a distraction and my gigantic hand is on full display.

"Oh, you poor thing, what happened to your hand?"

"Nothing of consequence," I reply.

"Is it painful?"

Now I think about it, I realise that it is throbbing. "Yeah, it's a bit sore."

"Oh, it must be getting you down. Explains why you seem so distant. Tell you what, give me your hand."

She digs in her monstro-handbag, which looks ready to set sail with a crew of 40 on a gay cruise. Next thing I know I can hear a *click, click,* then a spraying sound like deodorant. I look down. The bandage is speckled with little gems and glitter.

"What do you think?" she asks.

"Er, it's unique. Er, thanks."

The bell rings and I stand up, fast.

"Well, lovely to meet you..." Lila says. The line hangs as a question. I realise I never introduced myself.

"Thanks, Lila."

\*

The girl in front of me looks tough and I regret not making a run to the john to scrape off the sparkly decorations which aren't making me look exactly manly. She's wearing a leather jacket and drinking bourbon.

She has lots of black eyeliner and a tattoo of a black rose on the left side of her neck. I suspect under her T-shirt she's probably got a nipple ring.

I realise I'm gazing at her boobs and hastily move my eyes to her face. As I look at her, she stares back. It's a hard, unsettling look.

"I'm Pete," I say, nervously.

"Charlie," she says, still staring. Perhaps along with the nipple ring, she's hiding a knife. I squirm a little and scratch my nose.

Damn, I realise that I've unveiled my giant finger, in all its bejewelled glory.

She drops a scornful look at my bandage. "Lila?" She sounds mildly sympathetic. "She got to every guy that's been here. That girl needs to get a life."

"She thought it would cheer me up. It's a bit sore, you see." Surely this will soften her up.

"Poor you." She looks down at her cuticles, unimpressed. "What happened anyway?"

"Got in a fight."

She looks up. "Oh, yeah?"

"Yeah, two of them." I improvise. "Said they didn't like my haircut."

"Gotta say, can't blame them." Charlie eyes my painstaking I-just-got-out-of-bed locks. "Were they Russian?"

"Huh?"

"The guys? One with a blond moustache that doesn't match his hair and another with a scar on his forehead?"

"Uh, maybe."

"I think I know them – Selleck and Potter. They've got a thing about hairstyles. I'll introduce you," she decides. "It's the only way. They don't pick on people

172

they've talked to."

"Oh... OK."

"What do you do to protect yourself? You're tall, but weedy, so probably not weights or boxing. I do Krav Maga, but you don't look too coordinated. Maybe a weapon?" She digs around in her bag and pulls out a black business card with 'Eli's' slashed across it in red. "Go see Eli, he's the man. I'm thinking maybe a combat knife."

"Not big on knives right now," I comment, mindful of my aching finger.

"Maybe some nunchucks? Brass knuckles?"

"I'll think about it."

*

The next girl has a cute dimple on her left cheek, but it makes the stuff caked on her face sort of crack when she smiles. Her cheeks are a bit puffed out and she has these weirdly long, thin ears. Her face is a collection of fascinating things to look at.

I don't notice the white dress and long satin gloves at first. Her mouth is moving, her lips a deep red that wiggle like a graphic equaliser. When I eventually tune in, it's to her saying, "June is the ideal month. Not too hot but the spring chill gone from the air."

"June? Of course," I agree, mesmerised by her eyebrows, waggling as she talks. Belly-dancing caterpillars.

"I want one of those marquees, the ones you see at a circus, but tasteful, you know? But that's after the church. I don't actually go to church, so we'd have to start going, for a while, to convince the priest. It's Greek orthodox. Grand. Lots of marble and gold. Don't suppose you speak Greek?"

June. Church. Priest. Marquee. Oh shit. I pick my beer up with my right hand, deliberately.

Her eyes fall on my finger. "I think I'd go for more of an ivory bandage, to match the dress. Or we could dye it lilac to match the flowers. Yeah, that works."

Fuck.

"The good news is that it's your index finger, and your right hand. If it was your left ring finger it might give some people the idea you had commitment issues," she giggles. "Of course, we'll have to think up a respectable story to tell my parents. How did you do it, anyway?"

"Punched my girlfriend," I say, adroitly. She looks at the table and traces her fingers around the whorls in the wood.

"Well, no doubt she deserved it?"

"Probably. Had to ask her to change the channel. She can be slow like that."

"Perhaps anger-management training? Father's plenty able to afford it for you."

Ding. I love that sound.

*

The girl at next table has skin so pale it's almost translucent. She wears a flowing flowery dress that is also, interestingly, practically see-through. She's pretty. I perk up.

Gallantly, I kiss her on the cheek. A lovely smell hovers around her; it makes me think of raspberry-ripple ice-cream. She blushes. It's cute. "I'm Pete."

"Belle," she replies, her voice the chime of a fork on a wineglass.

"Belle," I say, "that's nice." Excellent, my mojo is returning. "What do you do for fun, Belle?"

"I adore forest clearings," she tinkles. "That's where they gather. At dusk, they come from the trees and dance into the long grass."

"They?"

"The fairies."

"You're a fairy watcher? As in people dressed up with wings and stuff?" Some people watch battle re-enactments, some gymnastics, I guess it's not that strange to watch fairies.

"They twirl and sing. It's beautiful. I love to watch them fly away, their yellow lights getting smaller as they shrink, to the size of an apple, and go to sleep in the trees."

"Oh, so it's a computer game?"

"No. The fairies. In the trees." She's speaking slowly now. "There's a lovely spot in the Dales they're fond of. You should visit."

She wafts her arm in the air, and her bracelets jingle. When she brings her wrist to the table again, I somewhat rashly reach out and touch the charms hanging off a chain. This brings my finger into view. She brushes her fingertips across the bandage. "Lovely," she almost sings, "magical." She blows on it, sending a puff of glitter into the air. "For good luck. Does it hurt?"

"A bit," I say.

Belle strokes my finger again. "You know, Esmeralda could mend this for you. She's generous with her gift."

"Esmeralda?"

"Yes, the healer of the local charm of fairies. Not far from here."

"So," I say, "you actually believe fairies are real?"

"Of course. Don't you?" I gape at her. Fairies. I had a

mate who went home with a girl who said she was a vampire. At least vampires are kind of sexy.

*

We get a bar break at this point.

"Listen, mate, I'm going to get off," I tell Nigel.

"That bad?"

"Look, I'm tired. I just…"

Nigel gives me a pleading look. It's less puppy dog and more demon headmaster. All the same, it makes me pause. Worst of all, Nigel does something I've never seen him do before. He begs. "Please, Pete. It's only another hour or so."

I remember the time Nigel trawled around all those pet shops with me, carrying Mr Zoot's corpse in his pocket so we could find just the right hamster replacement. To this day, he's never told Millie that Mr Zoot died in my care. "OK," I say and down the whiskey.

*

We bump shoulders before heading off. I'm clutching my whiskey as if it's a Fabergé egg. I generally avoid spirits but the floaty vortex swirling around me is comforting right now. I wish I was at home on the sofa, battling a can of John Smith's and watching re-runs of *MasterChef*.

The next girl twists awkwardly to look up at me. The first thing I see is the neck brace, similar to those collars they put on before you're airlifted to hospital.

Her keys sit next to her pint; she's ready to do a runner. I lump my hand onto the table, beyond caring. She looks at my hand as I stare at her neck.

We both start at once. "What happened to—" but we don't finish, both questions lost in our growing grins. She smiles like she's just thought of a dirty joke.

I squint down at the table, suddenly a bit shy. My gaze falls on her keyring, which reads: *I cook therefore I am*. I look back up, into her gingerbread eyes, framed by waves of pale, pale blonde locks. I want to know everything about her. I want her to know everything about me.

I watch as she brushes her hair behind her ear, and a single silver strand drifts onto the table between us.

Every cloud.

~

## Rachel McHale's Biography

I wrote my first novel when I was six years old. *The Amazing Panda Roo Roo* was a big hit with my audience of Mum and Dad. It was self-illustrated and stapled together on the right-hand side because I am a proud left-hander.

I'm a big fan of the short story form, with a particular interest in speculative fiction. Over the last few years my work has been placed or shortlisted in a number of competitions including the Bridport Prize 2017. Find out more on my website: www.rachelmchale.com

When I'm not moonlighting as a writer, I work as a nurse, and daydream about snow and skiing. I am currently studying for a Masters in Creative Writing in the beautiful city of York, UK.

# THE MONDAY NIGHT CLUB

*Shortlisted story, by Philip Charter*

A university professor, a gay rights activist, a sewage farmer, a sailor, a pensioner and a barmaid, walked into a bar. This is not a joke.

Although most of us were desperate for a drink, our 12-step program was not Alcoholics Anonymous, but instead a three month course: The Art of Writing Creatively. Back in the very first lesson, they had stressed the importance of avoiding adverbs, which was clearly lost on whoever named the bloody thing.

For us old codgers, each day is similar — buy a paper, take your pills, then submit several written complaints to the local borough council. Still, I thought I'd encounter more like-minded cantankerous folk at the start of the week, so I settled for a Monday course. As a 75-year-old widower residing in a London studio flat, I needed to find an outlet for my grumblings, and the classes were a darned sight cheaper than joining a lawn bowls club.

Rather than studying how to craft stories and beautiful verse, we learned to deflect blows and develop thick skins. By the end of each session, my tongue was sore from being bitten, and while the rest of the group were unpublished writers, they saw themselves as expert critics.

During the course I didn't learn where to appropriately employ the semi colon (in truth; nobody knows), but no matter who you share your miserable Mondays with, I learned that words need to be chosen with due care, and shared with extreme caution.

Before we toddled off to the bar, we had our final session in the classroom. Samuel was reading from his latest sexually charged diatribe.

"I moaned in unbridled ecstasy as he caressed my inner thigh. The flaming sun blazed through the open window, into my tempestuous heart..."

"Very powerful, Samuel," the tutor offered. "Perhaps you might remember that a lot of publications don't accept erotica, though."

"It's not erotica," he said. "You're just shocked it's two men."

"No, no. Only that it's important to embrace the emotive elements of your writing. Study feelings, not features."

The tutor, MArcus – a trendy polytechnic literature professor – spoke almost exclusively in meaningless alliteration. He told us to be less 'literal' and more 'literary', or more 'discursive' and less 'descriptive'. It's not a typo. MArcus let us know at every opportunity that he studied his MAsters at Stanford, under the tutelage of the MAsterful Tobias Wolff.

In all honesty, everyone else was sick of Samuel's agenda too. His readings transformed the classroom into a Soho dive bar, except without the possibility of guilt-free sex. We watched his T-shirts get tighter every week, stretched over his belly, with his bearded head bobbling on top. He announced in one session that he was in transition from *cub*, to *bear*. I had no idea what this meant, but refrained from asking him if that meant he now shat in the woods.

Samuel was by no means the worst storyteller in the group. Rita, the quick-witted barmaid, treated us to a series of tales about Jack the Ripper's brother, who didn't even murder anyone. Another torturous experience was suffering through Executive Assistant Gail's stories. She read her pieces with the clarity and precision of someone who expected us to take detailed notes. I did try once, but I lost the thread with her list of bizarre character names – Finkel Brunardi, Penelope Skylark, Marmaduke Beaujolais III.

When I read my poem, the hounds lay ready to attack, waiting for MArcus to give the first critique.

*...A lone passenger,*
*My thoughts stuck in neutral.*
*Dashboard lights blinking,*
*Some kind of secret message.*
*The engine turning over,*
*And out.*

*The belt had tightened and torn in,*
*Your heart, crumpled steel.*
*May you rest in pieces,*
*On the hard shoulder of my memory.*

"Was it about the car or an accident?" said MArcus.

"The loss of life."

"You sounded more concerned about the loss of your no-claims bonus, Duncan."

A few of the others tittered. I closed my notebook in defence.

"I think it's because you mentioned all of the parts of the car," said Gail, checking her notes and giving her expert opinion.

Being deaf in one ear often helps me ignore criticism, but I was proud of that poem, I'd spent days tinkering with it, tuning it up.

"It's not a complete write-off," said Samuel, "I'm sure you can fix it."

MArcus looked on, grinning. "Hey, do you know the last thing to go through Princess Diana's mind?" he asked. "...The engine."

An agonising silence followed. We all tried to ignore his raised eyebrows.

The classroom was part of a drab adult education complex in Holborn, where theatre shows go to die, and cafés sell falafel burgers for £16.95. They seemed to have a policy of removing anything art-like from the walls, and kept the strip lights at nuclear brightness.

By the evening, all that was left in the cafeteria were sad egg sandwiches and stewed tar coffee. Signs at every table reminded us that the staff would remain vigilant against the introduction of 'outside foodstuffs'. If they did smell something fishy, it was probably the tinned mackerel that I ate in the foyer each week.

Gail's detailing of the dark arts of waste water disposal never helped whet the appetite anyway. "In fact, *sewage* is the unprocessed household discharge, and *sewerage* is the system of distribution and filtration networks," she dictated, in her 1980s power suit with a blouse that looked like a tossed salad. Her hair was so wiry it could have removed even the toughest stains from a tray of baked lasagne. Cillit Bang, move over.

Back in class, Paddy did his best to help repair my broken ego. "'The belt had tightened and torn in...' It's a poem about a person. Do you really think it is an ode to a Volkswagen Golf?"

Paddy was another fascinating regular, an aspiring playwright who spent six months of the year transporting leathery millionaires around in their oversized bathtubs, and the other six twiddling his thumbs and presumably eating spinach. He had a handsome face, ruined by a nose that looked like it belonged to a roast dinner. Sometimes I felt like we were the only ones trying to keep the classes afloat, bailing out water while everyone else continued to pick holes.

Rita raised her make-up laden face. "It could be Empty Seat, like the Spanish car brand," she said with a wink.

Even I smiled at that one.

After class we walked into 'said bar', the whole rag-tag bunch. It was a characterless chain pub, which smelled of olive oil and extra-marital guilt. MArcus was doing his best to trap Rita (who was 20 years his junior and way out of his league), in his web of literary cleverisms, talking about the latest anthology he hoped would take off. We all hoped that he would take off.

"Who even invited him?" she hissed, coming back

from another toilet trip. "I wish he'd take a hint and go."

"Join the club," said Paddy.

"I suppose I already have."

MArcus oozled his way over to the group, with his smug glass of port and his cashmere jumper.

"So who'd like to sign up for the advanced course?"

"Is that to learn how to write fantastically creatively brilliant stories?" I asked.

No reply.

"Rita, I'd like to speak to you about something," said MArcus, breaking the silence. "In private."

"You can tell me here, it's fine," she said, clearing the blonde hair from her face.

"It's a scholarship option. Let's go to the bar, come on."

Rita gripped her chair like a cat avoiding a trip to the vet. The others sipped their drinks.

"Listen, Marcus," I said. "I think we know what is going on."

"Whatever do you mean, Duncan?"

"She's happy with us here. Just leave the girl be."

He set down his leather briefcase. "Well who asked you, Granddad?" he muttered.

"Pardon?"

"I don't even know why you bother," he said. "I've got my whole writing career ahead of me. You've got 10 years, at most."

This man needed to be put in his place, and I don't mean back in the fellows' smoking room at The University of the Uninspired. I took him to one side.

"Granddad has some bad news for you. He's already sold more books than you ever will."

He finished his port casually. "What's that?"

"Well, I haven't been completely honest." I said, putting a hand on his turtleneck shoulder. "My name's not Duncan. It's Dylan. Dylan Bainbridge."

"What are you talking about?" he scoffed. "Dylan Bainbridge?"

"Yes, Dylan Bainbridge. Costa Breakthrough Writer last year. Have you heard of *The Long Hard Road*?"

And with that, the student had become the master. It's funny that the identities of most successful authors, remain hidden on the inside of a book jacket. Nobody cares what you look like, unless you are 'multicultural' or 'sexy', or J.K. Rowling, and I'm certainly none of those things.

He slumped onto a nearby stool. "But that was a bestseller, half a million copies. Why are y—"

"Oh, the class?" I said. "Well, established authors can be such tortured souls, it's much better sharing your thoughts with real people."

He looked back at me open-mouthed.

This was the first time that MArcus had been lost for words since 1997 (which, he boasted, was the only time he'd ever suffered from writer's block). He just shut down like a cheap laptop and stood at the bar, his face a blue screen of death. After a few seconds, his self-preservation code kicked in and he grabbed his bag and went. He was a robot who had forgotten how to walk, bumping into a couple's table, sending their nibbles into complete disarray. MArcus 3,000 bleeped some kind of apology and wheeled off.

I had never planned to tear off my mask like some kind of decrepit superhero, but I got more satisfaction from that one moment, than I have from any book signing, or awards gala. Does that make me sound callous? Well, a lifetime of nobody listening, followed by everybody hanging on your next 120,000 words can make you a little cynical.

Lying to them all every Monday was the biggest rush I've had since I accidentally stole a Curly Wurly from the newsagent, and that was last century. But even with my less-than-subtle poetry, I found that I'm good at hiding in plain sight. Reeling off a pack of lies each week and having people believe you isn't all that hard. It's all just fiction.

~

## Philip Charter's Biography

Philip Charter is a writer who lives and works in Pamplona, Spain. He is tall, enjoys travel, and runs the imaginatively named website 'Tall Travels'. He spends a lot of time explaining the difference between 'fun' and 'funny' to his students, who occasionally refer to him as one of them.

# THE PLAN

## Shortlisted story, by John Emms

"But I don't want to breed with you."

Major Adams sighed. He hadn't expected this difficulty.

"But that's what you signed up for. The breeding crew. We need a new generation for when we arrive."

"Yes, but I didn't realise you'd be so, well, unattractive."

"That's not the point."

Sharon turned away, petulantly.

Adams wondered why none of the meticulous planning had catered for this. He'd assumed that being flight commander would make him... well, to be honest it had simply never occurred to him that anyone would be reluctant.

The flight was the first of several to Proxima B, the first exoplanet to be colonised by man. As commander he had many duties, but only one was shared by all those on board – to produce a new generation quickly, who would grow up and be in their early 20s on arrival. And for a significant number, including Sharon, that was their only duty.

"Anyway, why can't I do anything interesting?"

"That was all explained. The interesting things are all the responsibility of experts. People who are leaders in their field. Anyway, isn't producing and bringing up the first generation of young men and women to be born off the Earth interesting enough?"

"No. I want to help drive the spaceship."

"Drive it? Tell me, do you understand the spaceship?"

"I could learn."

"OK. So what do you think is powering us?"

"Pardon?"

"What's making us move?"

"Oh, I don't know. Some special kind of stuff? Hydrogen? Epsom salts?"

"See? You've no idea. We're powered by light."

"What?"

"Light."

"Oh. Well. Anyway, I may not know all that, but I don't know how a toaster works, either, but I can still make toast."

"OK. We'll let you make toast occasionally. But we have experts to, er, drive the spaceship. Just as we have experts in everything else we need. They do their jobs for which they're ideally suited. You do your job for which, may I say, you are also ideally suited."

"Oh. Am I?"

"Of course. Why else were you chosen? For the breeding crew we need people who are, well, I'm not sure how to put it, but it's definitely you."

"I think the word you're looking for is 'shaggable'."

"No it isn't. Or rather, well, yes, that describes the concept I had in mind, but..."

"That's sexist that is."

"No it isn't. It's all part of the plan. It's not just women in the breeding crew. It's half men, too."

"Oh, really?"

"Yes, of course. There's one in the next cabin? Called Rocky, I believe. Have you met him? He's been allocated to Professor Lucy Goldstein."

"So why can't I have one of them? A shaggable one. Like Rocky. He's gorgeous."

"This was all explained. The breeding crew breed with the expert crew. That way, statistically, we should finish up with a new generation of about half intelligent expert material, and about half, as it were, proletarian. Just what will be required."

Sharon pouted.

"Well, I still don't want to do it with you. Why didn't they appoint a shaggable commander?"

"Because I was appointed for my expertise. Breeding, for me, is a secondary duty. For you it's primary. Indeed, it's your only duty. So you need to be well qualified."

"It isn't my only duty."

"Isn't it? What other duties do you have?"

"Making toast."

There was a disturbance outside, then the cabin door burst open and a young, extremely muscular man stumbled in, impeded by a small, angular lady who was hanging onto his arm, trying to drag him back.

"Hey. You. Are you the flight commander?"

Adams spun round and stared at him.

"Yes, I am. Who the hell are you?"

"I'm Rocky Stallone. And I want to know why this gruesome broad is saying I have to screw her."

Professor Goldstein, for she it was who was trying to restrain him, bridled.

"Don't call me a broad."

"Lucy…" Adams clutched at his head. "What's going on?"

"We seem to have an unanticipated problem, major."

"Yes, I was beginning to find out for myself."

Stallone had turned his attention from the major and was staring at Sharon.

"Say, baby, where did you spring from?"

He moved towards her and slipped an arm round her waist. Sharon giggled and snuggled up to him.

"Leave her alone, Stallone."

"Oh yeah? Who's gonna make me?"

The major considered his own lack of stature and brawn against the copious amounts of both which had been allocated to Stallone, who now spat accurately on the floor between the major's feet.

"Come on, baby," he said, leading Sharon through the door and into the next door cabin. The door slammed behind them.

Adams turned to the professor, who was standing looking a little confused. He took her arm and led her towards the neatly made bunk.

"Slight change of plan," he said.

~

## John Emms's Biography

After a career got in the way, John Emms found time to write again after retiring. Since then, a number of short stories and articles, usually humour based, have featured in various publications. He has also, bizarrely, published a lengthy but entertaining (honestly...) history of local government lawyers. Also writes plays, a few of the shorter of which have won prizes or been selected for performance at a variety of venues around Yorkshire and Lancs.

JUDGES' STORIES

# CRAIG AND JENNIFER

*Judge's story, by Crystal Jeans*

Let me tell you a story about mutual love.

There was once a woman called Jennifer and a man called Craig. Jennifer was a hairdresser from Llanrumney. At five-foot-three and 11 stone she was a little on the fleshy side and her teeth were nicotine stained. Despite this, every single one of her male friends had thought about taking her to bed at some point. Some had even thought themselves in love with her. She had a certain charm. She was kind.

Craig hailed from Roath and he spent his days

painting bleak landscapes littered with bleeding stilettos. He was an artist. He had delicate cheekbones, permanent stubble and wore his long hair scooped into a bun. Craig was a man so secure with his sexuality that he was unafraid to wear eyeliner. All of his female friends had thought about taking him to bed at some point, and most had been granted their desires.

Craig and Jennifer met for the first time one cold November evening in the fruit and vegetable aisle of Tesco. Jennifer was placing sprouts into a plastic bag. She found one that looked all wrong – browning edges, small black holes in the outer leaves – and her first instinct was to smell it. Craig was passing by at this moment. He was stoned. When he saw this woman raise a small brown sprout to her nose, almost in slow motion, he felt a surreal thrill. He wanted to paint this moment. His foot collided with the edge of Jennifer's trolley. He tripped up and his armful of mangoes thudded to the floor. One of them landed on Jennifer's foot. She let out a, "Whoop," (adorable) and dropped her sprouts on the floor. They skated around like marbles and bounced off the twitching mangoes.

Craig had time to think the textures and colours of the fruit and veg poignant yet almost chilling; it brought to mind the pseudo-metanarratives of Russian dada and possibly the... God, her eyes. He knelt down. Jennifer had the same idea. Their heads banged together, hard. They both recoiled with identical expressions of pain and shock. Then laughed, blushing.

It was all very cinematic.

They talked for 10 minutes, the mangoes and sprouts still on the floor. Jennifer had fancied men at first sight before, but nothing like this. He was like a sexy Gareth Bale and she didn't care what any of her friends said about man-buns. Craig explained that he was buying mangoes to put in a kefir smoothie because he'd recently become interested in nutrition, after many years of living on noodles. Jennifer told him the sprouts were for her mother, for Sunday's roast. She felt it necessary to put this distance between herself and the sprouts.

Two hours later and Craig was bestowing the gift of cunnilingus to a lusty-eyed Jennifer on the paint-splattered floor of his living room. Afterwards they held each other very tightly and felt a closeness that they had never felt with other people, not even long-term lovers. There was a sexual chemistry and something else – they couldn't put their finger on it. Something to do with fate maybe, though that was ridiculous airy-fairy bollocks. Jennifer, insecure about her body, had always wrapped the duvet around herself to go to the toilet when in the company of men, but not with Craig. On the second day she was chasing him around the bedroom and slapping him in the face with her breasts while laughing hysterically. On the third day they stopped holding in farts and started comparing belly button odour. It was strange – that they could be their obscene selves but still find each other maddeningly sexy.

Jennifer stayed at Craig's place for four days before returning home. She told herself that it couldn't yet be love, it was too early for that, but her slow beaming smile said otherwise. Craig knew it was love on the third day but he kept this to himself.

All in all it was mutual.

From then on they were a couple, a fantastic couple – the sort that makes older, married people roll their eyes, smile, and say, "I remember when we were like that, George." And they both knew that neither loved the other any more or less. Craig didn't feel the need to play the usual mind games with Jennifer because he trusted, with his whole heart, that she wanted him entirely. He replied to her texts immediately and put three hearts at the end, one small, one big, one small. Jennifer responded in kind, adding emoticons of kittens blowing kisses. Craig hated emoticons. But not when Jennifer sent them.

Their friends didn't get it. Craig liked listening to Nick Drake and Belle and Sebastian, sometimes dipping into old school hip-hop when he wanted to impress certain people. Jennifer loved Beyoncé and Katy Perry. Craig wore paint-spattered corduroy and Jesus sandals. Jennifer had spray tans once a month. Craig read books that Jennifer would need a dictionary to get through – she'd dropped out of school at 16 and cared not for lofty ideas. Her favourite books were the Harry Potter series. Craig was that rare mix of pretentious and down-to-earth, and had to admit that J K Rowling could write a bloody good story and, in fact, he hadn't been able to put down the last one. When his friends looked at Jennifer with bemused, what-the-fuck-is-he-doing eyes, Craig deduced that this was all about class, and fuck them.

Both began to think that their friends were less important than previously considered.

They excelled at making love. They would go at it slow and, positions allowing, peep into each other's eyes with 'love me love me fuck me fuck me' faces, and the word that would come to their minds afterwards would be 'intense'. But some nights they fucked. Some nights Jennifer pissed onto his chest. Or explored his prostate. Either way, it would end the same every time

– with them wrapped around each other, stroking each other's faces and talking in baby voices, and then saying how they never thought they would end up being the type of twat who talked in baby voices, but adding, smiling, that since they were doing it with irony, it was OK. Everything was OK for *them*.

They had been together just over a year when Valentine's day arrived. Both, being cynical, had their doubts about the event (except for Jennifer who only pretended to have her doubts about the event), but they still wanted to celebrate it in some way because, well, how could they not? They agreed to go to town, split up for an hour, and buy each other two presents. One must be sweet and heartfelt, the other naff and cheap. Such a duality of expressions would clearly demonstrate their ambiguous (and superior) attitude toward the day. So they set out. Craig found a beautiful silver and amethyst bracelet that he knew Jennifer would love. She bought him a set of sabre paintbrushes and had the clerk burn his initials, C.G. into the wood. As for the naff gifts, both knew exactly what they wanted. And they both had the same idea. Craig bought a bag of sprouts from the market and Jennifer bought four fresh mangoes from Lidl. Each thought themselves a genius and a comedian.

They met up and agreed to open the presents when they got home, perhaps over a bottle of wine. Because it was a clear, crisp day, they decided to walk home.

They were so in love.

They headed towards Craig's place, hand in hand, enjoying the cloudless sky and the unusually mild winter weather. Jennifer was thinking about the fact that the first time the love of her life saw her she was sniffing a mouldy sprout – talk about sexy – and Craig was imagining fucking his beloved over the kitchen table. Anally. They crossed the road, half in a dream. They heard the sound of a fast approaching car at the same time. Their heads snapped around. They were in the middle of a road and there was a dark blur of a car racing toward them, fast. Was the driver drunk? It had appeared out of nowhere. Was this the end? Of their lives and their love? What about their future children, little Jarvis and Lucy, what about the Labrador, Mavis, who would sleep at the end of their bed and make funny little noises in her sleep, what about *everything*?

Craig's first and only instinct was to protect Jennifer, to push her out of the way. She was worth dying, or at least getting seriously injured, for. But because their love was perfectly mutual, Jennifer had the same idea. Their heads smacked together with a bony thud and this time they didn't have the time to find each other's eyes and laugh because the car, the mad lunging car with its mad stupid driver, came upon them and threw their bowling pin bodies into the air. The bags they had been carrying followed them, into the windscreen, over the side, and onto the ground.

As Craig and Jennifer lay together on the cold tarmac, their dark blood oozing out, four perfectly ripe mangoes and a handful of sprouts skittered around them like marbles before reaching a dead stillness.

~

## Crystal Jeans' Biography

Crystal Jeans is the author of *The Vegetarian Tigers of Paradise* (Honno Press), which was shortlisted for the Polari Prize 2017, and *Light Switches are My Kryptonite* (also Honno), which won Wales Book of the Year in the English fiction category. She lives in Cardiff with a small blonde gremlin.

~

# Crystal's Competition Judging Comments

Excellent selection here, was really tough choosing the best. Luckily I enjoy judging people. The hardest part was choosing between stories that were brilliantly written but not hilarious, and those that were funny but not as well-executed. Many managed both. All were fab reads. Well done, shortlistees.

# COLLECTING SHELLS

*Judge's story, by Edward Field*

We collect shells, my family and me. It's not most people's bag, but it's our *thing*. We'd never bring anyone else. Some things can't be shared. Sunday mornings are best, when the beaches are quietest; when families not like ours are still scoffing breakfast in bed with their newspapers. We suffer the company of early dog walkers and the beachcombers looking for washed-up treasure and whale puke, but mostly they've learnt to keep their distance. They only invade our space once. Strangers are quick learners around my family.

Autumnal beaches are best. The mornings aren't too dark, but the wind is up and whips the sand away so we can see tips of the shells. It's better if we don't have to dig for them. Careless spades and probing fingers risk too much damage. And you don't want to stand on them. Not if you want something left to see afterwards. You wouldn't believe what dogs and owners can do with their great clodhopping feet. In my 14 years, I've seen more careless destruction on the beach than most people will see in 20 lifetimes.

I know what you're thinking: *Once you've seen one shell, you've seen 'em all*. But, trust me, every one is different. I've been doing this my whole life, so I should know. Each one has its own secrets and stories about its journey to wherever we find it. Sometimes they're clean – not like new-born, but definitely not like they've spent yonks in the wild and dangerous Great Outdoors – but mostly they're dirty with oil, grit and hitchhikers covering them: tiny limpets and clusters of mussels hanging on to the dents and ridges, or seaweed tangled, dried and sticking to the surfaces that are pitted and roughed up by all the years under the sand or bashed by the millions of pebbles the sea chucks at them. It's amazing there are any left intact for us to find, when you consider what they've been through.

I used to be astonished by some of the places we found them, but nothing surprises me now. It's not only on beaches, like you'd expect. We've found them on the cliff paths, buried under gorse bushes and even once on a farm, miles from anywhere. *Honest.* That was our most exciting find ever. Mum found that one. We couldn't believe it was still there and in such good nick after all those years of cows and tractors thundering over it. Imagine if they'd ploughed that field. Game over.

We keep our Finders Chart on the fridge, held on with magnets from seaside resorts we've searched. Mum's in the lead, of course, and Dad's still in second place, but I reckon I'll catch up with him soon, now that he mostly supervises. I'll move into third place before too long, for sure. It only takes one brilliant day out there. And with Toby away at boarding school now, I've got a clear run most weekends.

When you find one, you have to shout out straight away and ID it if you can. Everyone gathers round to confirm the 'find' and you get an extra bonus point if your ID is spot on. Dad checks the photos in the book and, if he concurs, Mum puts the score in her notebook ready for the Finders Chart. Even after all these years there're a few we're not sure of. *You* try learning every shell in the book.

You have to shout loud and clear 'cos we're usually quite spread out. "Got one," is usually my shout. With Toby it's something corny like, "The dude does it again," or, "Strike one for gold." Dad thinks he's funny when he yells, "Guess what I've found," like there'll be a pot of gold under his nose. Mum lets loose with her banshee scream that always makes me laugh and scares the hell out of any 'publics' who've strayed too close.

Today, I'm first to hit pay dirt.

"Mine," I shout.

It isn't ownership that I'm claiming. Since Dad lost both arms and half his face, we've learnt to be wary. After so many years, mines are a rare treasure. It's a miracle there are any left after all these years, and this one's gotta be worth double points, for sure. But I still prefer the shells; fragile, corroded, holding their secrets tightly inside. You can't know if they've rusted out and are duff now, or if they've clung on to life and are still primed to be a killer.

It's only when we place the tiny triggering charges around one, tether a puppy – or a sheep if there's one nearby – next to it and then run away that we know for sure. You don't *need* an animal, but without one you don't get the full experience. On the farm we used a cow, but it's not easy dragging one of those down to the beach on the off-chance.

You have to run fast. And far. The blast crater can be about 30 feet. On a good day, I've seen one almost 50. You can't hang about with something that big going off. I know we could run a wire out to it and hide behind a rock with a plunger like they do on the old war films, but where's the fun in that? Nah, we like the adrenaline rush of the sprint. I'm the fastest in my class at school now. I've practiced my dead-start sprints every day since we lost Maddie. She was only five, and misjudged it. With hobbies like ours, it's best to learn from other people's mistakes.

~

# Edward Field's Biography

Ed has spent much of 2018 writing, editing, judging, shortlisting and being highly commended and published, some of which may even be deserved. In common with a few of the writers who entered To Hull And Back 2018, this year has involved a healthy amount of cannibalism and murder. He is not currently admitting to specific instances but has become something of an expert at digging and is particularly proud of his tomato crop this year.

A more complete bio can be found on the pages of Chris Fielden's most excellent website, as well as Ed's own: www.squircle.me

~

## Ed's Competition Judging Comments

It's been a mixed bag of experiences judging this year's competition. Humour is such a subjective issue. Just look at Donald Trump; on a daily basis, quite frankly I don't know whether to laugh or cry.

At the time of writing this, I have no idea whether the other judges share my opinions on the winning stories. For me, I had three very clear winners and a fourth that was just a sigh or careless typo away from crashing the party. Whether, when the results are announced, I'll be chuckling with delight or grinding my teeth in horror that the others don't share my view of the stories' brilliance remains to be seen. But, anonymous authors, know this: I *really* enjoyed those four stories (and a few others) enough to read them several times.

I think the real joy in judging a short story or flash fiction competition is the possibility of reading something genuinely original, being hooked by a phrase or sculpture of words that stands out enough to be scribbled down, or wandering into a yarn that moves, repulses or thoroughly entertains me. And just occasionally, a story comes along that does all of the above. *That's* what I take from the judging process.

# EGGS

*Judge's story, by Christie Cluett*

Angela was carrying an egg around in her vagina. It fitted perfectly up inside her and she was able to walk around without any hindrance, but with the knowledge that it was there, protected inside her by flesh, blood and cervix.

She felt like a mother hen, at the office, at home, on the bus, during squash games, at the cinema, eating chips, staring at strangers kissing. She felt like she had a purpose and, happily, she carried that egg everywhere, hands free. Until one morning.

While watching her neighbour mow his lawn with his top off, beads of sweat glistening on the hairs on his shoulders, she felt a dull pain in her abdomen.

"Oof," she said, exhaling in surprise at the pain. Then, resting a hand against herself, she heard a distinct *crack*. Her mouth formed a small silent 'o' as she stood at the sink, the sound of the mower distant.

She undid the buttons of her trousers and pushed them down over her hips, pulling down her pants just in time to catch a small, bright spot in the gusset – a yellow yolk, perfectly round. She watched it wobble as she shuffled to the kitchen table and carefully sat down.

As she did, holding her pants out by the elastic, the yolk burst and, from within, she saw something floating. Angela leaned closer, reaching down with a scouting finger to prod the something. Two small hands gripped hold of the end of her finger and she raised, from the yolk in her pants, a perfectly formed little man. He looked to be about 40 years old, with brown hair in a side parting and blue jeans.

"Hello," Angela said. "You're awfully small."

The small man nodded with an expression that suggested this was obvious, but Angela continued.

"I'll call you Jeff," she said and, ignoring his wriggles and muffled complaints, she popped him back into her vagina from whence he came.

~

## Christie Cluett's Biography

Christie writes comedy fiction and is currently making the final edits to her first novel, a dark comedy about anxiety and trying to be normal. She's one of the founding members of Stokes Croft Writers, excels at improvised nonsense and is learning to fly.

~

## Christie's Competition Judging Comments

I'm excited and honoured to be judging To Hull And Back for another year. It's a cliche, which Chris hates (little tip), but the entries really do get better every year. This year, the stories were inventive and charming, and my favourites were the ones with subtle humour told in an original way. Good luck to everyone who entered and roll on next year.

# MR KILL

*Judge's story, by Christopher Fielden*

1

Mrs Ida Wadworth is looking at me sceptically. I've explained that I can't resuscitate the dead worm she's produced from her pocket. She seems to be having trouble accepting my prognosis.

"But you're a vet," she says.

"No I'm not."

"It says so on your door."

"No it doesn't."

She surveys me with unmasked contempt. "Are you going to save my worm?"

"It's been cut in half."

"I know that, you fool. I did it with my trowel."

"Even if I were a vet, there is no way to reanimate a decapitated worm."

"So you *are* a vet."

"No. I'm a doctor."

Ida scrutinises me with rheumy eyes, her purple hair rinse glowing with alien phosphorescence. "You look like a vet to me."

I've run out of different ways to say the same thing. Thankfully, Ida moves towards the door. As she leaves, I receive a scowl 80 years in the making, but I discern a hint of disappointment in her glare, as though she had expected more from me. The door clicks shut behind her.

I sit for a minute and consider the patient I've just seen. Could she be a potential candidate for The Programme? No. She might be senile, but I enjoy Ida's visits. She isn't a bad person and, although rude, she often delivers the unexpected into an otherwise predictable day. With her walking its streets, the village of Dingle Green is a more interesting place to live.

As I turn back to my computer, I feel an intense pain in my head. It arrives from nowhere. I reach up to rub my scalp. As quickly as it materialised, the pain vanishes, as though it were never present. I investigate with my fingertips, half expecting to see blood, but there is nothing. Feeling slightly disorientated, I reach out and press the buzzer to summon my next patient.

The room shifts slightly, taking on a hazy quality. I wipe my forehead, but my skin is dry.

Looking back at my computer screen, I see most of the details for my next patient are missing. I click refresh. Now there's even less information.

I jump with surprise as I notice a man in the room, sitting on the chair Ida vacated. He's watching me intently. I didn't hear him enter the room, or notice any movement. I feel myself redden as though caught in the middle of some nefarious act.

The man is dressed in black, his leather coat long and worn. He has mutton chops on his cheeks, but manages to wear them more like Wolverine than John McCririck. His hair is dark and streaked with grey. Pallid skin is clamped tightly to his skull, making him look ill. In contrast, his stare burns with life. I find it unnerving.

"I'm afraid we're having some computer problems," I say. "Can I take your name?"

"Kill."

"I'm sorry?"

"Kill." The man's eyes are a piercing grey, the colour of stormy sky.

"Mr Kill... OK. Forename?"

"Slash."

Marvellous. A joker. Or a fruitcake. I hope he's the latter. It might mean he's eligible for The Programme.

"Middle names?"

"Hack, Maim."

"You expect me to believe your name is Slash Hack Maim Kill?" I look up and wish I hadn't. Mr Kill's expression indicates two things. One: He is indeed Mr Slash Hack Maim Kill. Two: If he's asked his name again, I might come out of this encounter one testicle down. "Your parents must have had a sense of humour."

He smiles thinly. "My old man likes Frank Zappa."

Now my computer screen is completely blank. "I'm sorry," I say as I pick up the phone. "Please bear with me." The phone's dead, too, and I notice the second hand on my clock has stopped moving. Have we had a power cut?

"I hear things," says Kill. I jump again, this time because his voice is so close. He's pulled his chair towards me, but I didn't see or hear a thing.

"Voices?"

"Kind of."

"Do they tell you things?"

Kill leans forward, as though to impart a dreadful secret. "The voices sing to me."

I feel my neck tingle with gooseflesh and simultaneously fight the urge to laugh. A picture grows in my mind of the devil singing a lullaby to this man, tickling his chin lovingly with a black, pointed talon.

"The voices are accompanied by guitars, bass and drums," Kill continues. "Amazing riffs, rolling rhythms, thundering bass lines. But recently the music has changed."

"How so?"

"The voices have started singing about you."

There's something about the way he imparts this information that makes me feel my life expectancy has diminished. The urge to laugh deserts me. "Me?"

"I know what you've done."

Done? What have I done?

"You know," he says.

Now I feel like I'm the patient and he's the doctor. I didn't say that out loud.

"No, you didn't. The voices that sing to me have become one – your voice. Lately it's been getting louder. Now it's so loud it's drowning out the rest of the band, and I'm a man who prefers instrumentals."

I wonder if I'm dreaming. No, dreams hold a certain recognisable quality, something that tells you, deep down, that it's just a dream. This is happening. The question I can't answer is: *What* is happening?

I fight an unfamiliar feeling. It takes me a while to recognise it as panic. My eyes are drawn to Kill's face. Who is this man? He arrived like a ghost. And he says he hears voices. Is he toying with me? Usually, people who hear things have some sort of mannerism: a twitch or social inability. The chilling thing about Mr Kill is his lucidity. Then, realisation strikes.

"You're not real."

"So why are you talking to me?"

I consider this. Maybe Kill is a figment of my imagination; I've been working a lot lately and feeling exhausted. I close my eyes for a few seconds and then open them. He's still there. I reach out and touch his arm. He feels solid, but there's something amiss. I turn his hand palm upwards and press my fingertips against his wrist bone, feeling for a palpitation of the radial artery.

"You have no pulse."

He nods, as if I'm stating the obvious rather than understanding the entire situation. "I don't need one." His stare bores into me like two spinning drill bits. "Neither do you."

I grab my wrist. There's no pulse. "I'm dead?" He nods. "Who the hell *are* you?"

"You know who I am."

I shake my head. "I'm dead so you've come for me?"

"No. You've come to me. Your body lies dead in your office. This is limbo, the place between life and death."

I can't take this in. I look around. "We're in my office."

"No. What we see around us is a reflection of the moment of your death. Look on it like a warehouse – a holding area for your spirit while I decide the manner of your deliverance."

"You're Death?"

"No. I'm Kill. Death is my father. Death waits for those who've died. I wait for those who've been killed."

"Killed..." He nods. "I was murdered?"

"Yes." His patience seems to be ebbing. Do I care? No. I'm dead. What can he do to hurt me now?

"You'd be surprised," he says.

I don't like that he can read my thoughts. I'm finding the lack of privacy unsettling.

"Get used to it."

I didn't know I was dead until Kill had spelled it out for me. How could someone kill me without me realising it?

"The killer was gifted. He planned and executed the murder perfectly." He gives me the drill stare again. "The problem with your Programme is you only considered the candidates and those they might harm. You failed to consider those who might be negatively affected by your actions. Remember your last kill?"

"Yes." It had saddened me, but she had to be stopped. She couldn't accept living with HIV, couldn't forgive the man that had infected her. Being pretty, she used her looks to seduce men and spread the disease. For her, it represented revenge.

"Her father is a retired soldier," said Kill. "He saw you leaving the scene. He decided to deal with you himself. Remember the sudden pain you felt in your head?" I nod. "It was a bullet."

I rub the back of my head. I can feel no wound. But then, if Kill is to be believed, I am no longer in my body.

I feel confused. Cheated. It all seems so unfair. "But my life's work isn't complete."

"Neither were the participants' in your Programme. I'm familiar with your work. I've met all your victims."

"Victims?" I spit the word. If he were truly familiar with The Programme, he'd realise there were no victims. More lives would be saved in the absence of the sadistic, selfish, twisted and cruel. And I always carefully consider each candidate, study them, making sure they're appropriate.

"True, but remember the banker?"

I look blankly at him. There have been so many...

"He liked to drink," continues Kill. "Killed a girl in a hit and run."

I nod. "He'd have done it again."

"He did. You murdered his twin."

Could I have made such an idiotic error? Surely not. I was meticulous. I always made sure.

"You tried, but everyone makes mistakes. Why did you think you wouldn't? Ironically, your arrogance would make you a candidate for your own Programme." A thin smile touches Kill's lips. I don't like it. He's laughing at me, not with me.

"So," I say, not hiding my irritation. "What happens now?"

His smile fades. "I shall ask you one simple question. Your answer will determine your path into the Ever." He reaches inside his jacket and pulls out two sickles. One has a shimmering blade of sunlight, the other is the colour of night. They sizzle as he moves them through the air. "Are you ready?"

For once I feel I know what's coming next and this

fills me with calm. The confusion I have experienced until now washes away. Kill's manner has changed. He knows I know. I am dead. Eternity awaits. Have I done wrong? No. I have saved countless lives with no expectation of recognition for my achievements. Should I give an answer I believe he wants to hear? No. I can't. He'd know I lied. All I can do is answer honestly. I'm ready for judgement.

"Do you admit doing wrong?"

"No. I did no wrong."

"I bid you farewell, Dr William Hatton."

Kill swings the two sickles. They plunge into my chest. There is no pain. Kill is gone. My office is gone. Everything is gone.

2

I'm in the dark. Damp earth presses around me. The feeling is pleasant. I'm content in the cold, wriggling forward, eating that which is in front of me, leaving that which is behind me. I feel safe.

Everything around me erupts. Cold metal rips into my midriff. Soil tumbles. Light dazzles. I feel a warm hand on my cold body. I wriggle, finding the heat distressing. A pair of rheumy eyes peer at me, surrounded by a halo of purple.

"Oh dear," says Ida Wadworth. "Don't worry, little worm, I know where to take you. If there's one man who can save your soul, it's Dr William Hatton."

~

## Christopher Fielden's Biography

I started running the To Hull And Back short story competition in 2013. When I launched it, I thought, *This is mental, no one will enter, I won't have to ride to Hull.*

I was right about one thing. It is mental.

The mathematicians among you will have concluded that only 33% of my assumptions were correct. Sadly, this level of accuracy seems to apply to all of my life decisions, which is probably why I have no money.

Since launching the competition, I've made the journey to Hull on the hog four times. That's about 2,000 miles with a book strapped to my bike, getting strange looks from other road users. See? Mental.

I plan to run this bad boy until I die. For a slightly podgy middle-aged man, my health isn't that bad, so To Hull And Back will probably be around for a while yet.

If you want to know more about me, the About page on my website contains more information than anyone could want to know:

www.christopherfielden.com/about/

~

## Chris's Competition Judging Comments

This year, I received a record number of submissions into the competition. The history of entry numbers looks like this:

- 2018: 456 (+97)
- 2017: 359 (+75)
- 2016: 284 (+68)
- 2015: 216 (+122)

- 2014: 94

The early bird fee made the reading more manageable this year. At the end of April 2018, I'd received 208 entries, compared to 124 entries in 2017. This accounts for 84 of the extra 97 entries this year, which has made the growth manageable.

The flow of submissions from May through to July was also more steady, so I managed to stay on top of the reading until mid-July. Still, there was a big influx of entries as the closing date approached – 187 in the final month, 110 in the final week, 38 on the final day. Last year, it was 170 in the final month, 100 in the final week and 26 on the final day. So similar(ish).

I know I say this every year, but I am NOT complaining about the amount of entries I receive – it's fantastic that so many people enter and support the competition. I'm extremely grateful and hope the number of entries continues to grow in the future. I simply share these stats because I find them interesting and it helps me find better ways of managing the reading process.

This year, I went to Wales to undertake the reading and judging. I visited my friends, Alison, Jim and Jackson, in Northwich. While I was there, Jackson drew me.

Got to say, he nailed it. Especially the amount of wrinkles. Thanks, Jackson...

After being deeply traumatised by Jackson's artwork, I headed to Ceibwr Bay in Pembrokeshire to recover. I spent a night there and then headed to Mwnt, in Ceredigion, just north of Cardigan. I did most of the reading in this location, then went to the Cambrian Mountains to make decisions.

The quality of the stories entered this year was staggering. I particularly enjoyed the inventiveness and use of imagination behind many of them – there were so many fresh ideas and storylines that I hadn't seen before. Reading them was inspiring.

I haven't made many changes to the 2019 competition. I decided to keep the word limit at 2,500. If necessary, I may drop the limit to 2,000 words in future years, just to help manage the reading. For now, it stays the same.

Here are the changes I did make:

1. Prize pot increased from £2,250 to £2,750:
    a. First: £1,000
    b. Second: £500
    c. Third: £250
    d. 3 x Highly Commended: £100 (up from £50)
    e. 14 x Shortlisted: £50 (up from £25)
2. Increased entry fees, to help cover the bigger prize pot and maintain growth:
    a. Early-bird entry fee – if you enter the competition before 30th April, you will pay £11 for one story, £18 for two stories, £22 for three stories
    b. If you enter between 1st May and 31st July, you will pay £13 for one story, £21 for two stories, £26 for three stories

I hope I'm not putting people off entering by increasing the fee every year. It's simply so I can increase the prize money for all the published writers, cover the costs and make the competition more prestigious.

Overall, I'm hoping the competition will break even again this year, but a small loss is possible (as always, it depends on anthology sales). Prizes are first £1,000, second £500, third £250, 3 x runner-up £50 and 14 x shortlist prizes £25 – total £2,250. Other costs include PayPal, video production, admin, website maintenance, publishing the anthology, advertising, putting on a book launch and, of course, the epic journey to Hull and back.

All the judges, artists and everyone else involved with the competition continue to give their time for free, which I appreciate greatly.

As I mentioned, next year's competition will have an increased prize pot. Last year, I increased the 2nd and 3rd prize, so I decided to concentrate on the 14 lower prizes this year. This means everyone that is published in the anthology will receive a bit more cash. Next year, if the competition continues to attract more entries, I will have to decide whether to up the top prize, or up the lower 14 prizes again. Something to think about... we'll see what happens.

As I've said before, the long-term aim is to provide a five figure top prize to help the competition become more widely known and give humorous short stories a respected publishing platform to be celebrated from. I'm continuing to explore the possibility of sponsorship. Maybe one day...

Entries this year came from an increasing number of locations around our fabulous planet. They include: Australia, Austria, Belgium, Canada, England, Finland,

France, Germany, Greece, Ireland, Israel, Italy, Jersey, Latvia, New Zealand, Nigeria, Northern Ireland, Romania, Scotland, South Africa, Spain, Sweden, Switzerland, Trinidad and Tobago, Turkey, USA and Wales.

This year, the number of writers who disobeyed the rules dropped substantially, to 37 (7% of the 456 entries) from 102 (28% of the 359 entries in 2017), which is great. Unfortunately, I still had to disqualify 16 stories, which is more than last year (11). Most of these were either over the word count limit, or failed to obey any of the rules.

If you weren't longlisted or shortlisted this year, please don't be disheartened. Each year there are more entries but the same number of places on the short and longlist. I don't reject stories because I don't like them. I simply select the stories that are best suited to this competition.

The judging process is highly subjective. Many of the stories entered will go on to be published elsewhere. If you haven't been successful in this competition, keep on submitting those excellent stories. If you keep your work under consideration, you will enjoy success.

That's it. Year five is done and dusted. To Hull And Back is half a decade old. I've read hundreds of stories. I've laughed a lot. I've been inspired, surprised and delighted by some brilliant writing. Thank you to everyone who has entered. I can't tell you how much your support means to me without sounding like an overly sentimental knob-head. But it really does mean a lot. Honest.

Cheers me dears, Chris.

# OFFICE MEAT

*Judge's story, by Mel Ciavucco*

It's 11:42. I'm absolutely starving. I just need to make it to midday, that's the earliest I can possibly get away with going for lunch without the others commenting. Karen regularly offers to staple my stomach for me, literally a do-it-yourself tummy-tuck with one of the office staplers. Oh, she's hilarious.

Blueberries for breakfast does nothing to fill you up. I had one rice cracker at 10:00. Rice crackers aren't even

221

real food, surely? I look at the clock in the corner of my computer screen. It's still 11:42. Maybe it's wrong. Can the time be wrong on my computer? A mix of panic and hope spread through me and I look at the time on my phone just in case. Nope. Still 11:42.

I glance around the room. Colin is leaning back in his chair on the phone saying lots of sentences that start with, "Well actually." Karen is staring intently at something on her desk. She's probably admiring her collection of staplers. Carol isn't in here. Wait, why? Is she in the kitchen? Surely she's not having lunch already? If she is, then I'm totally allowed to have mine. The bitch. She's probably gone to have a secret scoff. She's on Weight Watchers and is always boasting about losing two pounds that one time. Fuck Carol.

For the last week and a half, my new regime has been: get up at 05:00, go to the gym, go to work, watch *Love Island*, sleep, repeat. I wish I could eat a giant bar of Dairy Milk and drink an entire bottle of Pinot Grigio every night to forget about this soul-destroying office job, but I remind myself that I'll never look like the girls on *Love Island* if I do. Yesterday I cut out all the pictures of skinny women from all my magazines and stuck them on the fridge. I know they're photo-shopped but it still does a great job of reminding me that I'm a lard-arse. Not that my dad will ever let me forget that anyway.

Right, I'm just going to go for lunch. Who cares what they think, I'm too hungry. I push up to my feet. I actually feel a little dizzy. Oh God, I'm malnourished. Will I die? Well, I didn't die on the other diets – the 5:2 diet, the alkaline diet, even eating like a caveman on the paleo diet. It felt like I was going to die though. I quietly sneak around the desk, glancing at the others, who don't seem to notice.

"Lunch already, Jules?" Karen announces. "New diet hitting you hard, eh?"

*My fucking name is fucking Julie*, I say in my head. They've been calling me Jules for too long now, it'd be too awkward to correct them.

"Well, it's near enough 12," I say with a nervous giggle on my way to the door. I can feel her eyes on my back as I walk. She's judging me for being a greedy fat bitch, I just know it. She's probably holding back vomit at the sight of my wobbling, jelly-like arse.

In the kitchen, Carol – looking exactly what you'd expect the word 'mumsy' to be defined as in the dictionary – is making a cup of coffee.

"I didn't think it was lunchtime already," she says, looking me not-so-subtly up and down. Does she really think I don't notice when she does that? She is just the worst. She tuts in the afternoon when I eat my second rice cracker. She critiques everything I eat for lunch. She gives me tips on how to wear more flattering clothes to cover my tummy. I hate the word tummy, it's for five year olds.

"Been to the gym today?" she continues. "Hope you're working on toning those arms, you might be able to flap away with those wings otherwise."

My hands start curling into fists as she chuckles to herself.

Colin walks in. "Ladies," he announces as he goes to the fridge and pulls out a triple layered sandwich with mayonnaise oozing out against the cling film. He puts it on the table, along with the carrier bag in his hand. He takes out a can of Coke, a packet of crisps and a Yorkie bar.

"Some people prefer chocolate straight from the fridge," he tells us, "but I like it soft so it melts in the mouth more easily." He smacks his lips, a trickle of saliva sticking to his beard. He pulls the chair out – way out – he needs room for his belly. Nobody in the office gives a fuck what Colin eats. Nobody cares that he's fat.

"Well, lucky you," Carol says. "We ladies don't get to enjoy such things." She glances at me. "Jules has been doing so well recently on her diets." Her tone is so patronising, she's barely even trying. "You probably shouldn't be eating things like that in front of her, Colin. We wouldn't want her to break her diet now, would we?"

I grind my teeth and feel my nails press into my palms. *Food*, I think. *Just get the salad out of the fridge.*

I get my salad out of the fridge. I look at Colin as he takes a bite out of this humongous sandwich. I would literally kill to eat bread right now.

"Oh, good on you, Jules," says Karen, having appeared from nowhere.

Great, everyone's here now. "It's just salad," I blurt.

"Yes, but think of how slim and beautiful you are going to be."

"Can salads work miracles now?" laughs Colin.

What. Did. He. Just. Say.

"Just joking, love." He genuinely looks a bit scared. I must be doing some kind of death stare.

"Hey come on, it's just a joke," he says. "You know I think you're lovely just as you are. Us gentlemen like a cuddly woman. A bit of meat on the bones."

"Yes, what's that saying?" Karen says. "Only dogs like bones, real men like meat."

Like Karen would know. She's like one of those annoyingly small spare ribs from the Chinese takeaway, barely worth nibbling at for its tiny bit of flesh.

"There you go, Jules," Carol says. "Some men like a

voluptuous woman. You might still find Prince Charming after all."

The fire is rising within me and I feel like I'm going to burst. I mean, it could just be my stomach rumbling but I feel like it's saying, "Kill the bastards. Kill them *all*."

I take a deep breath. "I told you several times before," I say, trying to put on my stern voice, "I do not care if men fancy me. I do not fancy men." What don't they understand about that?

"Well," starts Carol, picking up her coffee. "What you do behind closed doors is your—"

"Nooooooo," I scream, no longer able to contain the rage. Jumping to my feet, I lunge towards her, knocking the coffee out of her hand, sending it flying all over Karen's blouse. I open my Tupperware box and tip the salad over Carol's head as she squeals, then I repeatedly bash her over the head with the Tupperware.

Karen is too busy crying about the coffee down her blouse. Colin is just sitting there with a mouthful of sandwich. I grab Carol by the hair and drag her over to the fridge. I open the fridge door and push her head inside, then repeatedly slam the fridge door over and over in her face. It feels incredible. Colin finishes chewing, jumps up and tries to grab me. I twist out of his grip and am surprised – or am I? – that he's still holding his sandwich.

"Fuck off, Colin," I shout.

I pick up one of the chairs and whack it hard around his head. It knocks him out. I stare at the chair, impressed with my strength.

Carol is groaning on the floor, her face turning shades of red and purple. Right. Karen. Where is that bitch? I grab some forks out the cutlery drawer and burst through the door into to the office. She's trying to hide behind a desk. Stupid cow.

"Karen?" I call. "Stand up and put your hands where I can see them."

She slowly stands up, her hands reaching up in the air, one of them holding a stapler. "Jules, listen—"

"My name is not fucking Jules," I scream as I run over to her. "It's Julie."

I grab the stapler out of her hand, put her pinky finger in it and press down hard.

"Ow," she says, though the staple didn't break the skin of course.

I push her over onto the floor and straddle her on the ground. She screams as I push one hand over her head and stab a fork into the middle of it, pinning it to the carpet. I do the same with Karen's other hand. I have one fork left. Karen's eyes widen as she screams and I see my opportunity. I tighten my grip on the fork and push it straight into her left eye. Her screams become shriller. I shake in amusement and wonder. I've seen it done in films, but in real life it's incredible. It went right through the eyeball. What would happen if I took it out now?

I yank on the fork and the whole eyeball comes out. I laugh in amazement. Karen is still screaming and jolting around, which is getting rather annoying. I move up and position my arse over her face so her screams are muffled. I stare at the eyeball, at the red tendrils hanging down and I remember how hungry I am. So fucking hungry. I lick the eyeball, just to see what it tastes like. It's kind of slimy but it doesn't taste of much. Fuck it. I pop the whole thing in my mouth. And pop it goes. Gooey mixture seeps out and fills my mouth. It's really not that different to eating sushi, I tell myself. I don't like sushi that much, but I'm so hungry. I suddenly wonder how many calories it has in it. No. Fuck calories. Fuck Karen. Fuck Colin and fuck Carol. Karen has stopped moving now. Finally. My fat arse is actually pretty handy at times.

I get up, grab the Sellotape off my desk and go back into the kitchen. This time, I get a knife out of the drawer. A sharp one, none of this butter knife malarkey. Carol staggers to her feet.

"Lunchtime's over," I say and stab her right in the gut. I push her over to the other side of the kitchen as she whimpers and slides down the wall.

Colin starts to groan as he comes to. Dragging him over to the table, I grab his hands, raise them above his head either side of the table leg and wrap Sellotape tightly around his wrists. I wrestle his kicking legs down and tape his feet together.

"Well, I'm so glad you like cuddly women, Colin. How jolly decent of you." I rip his shirt open, buttons popping all over the linoleum floor. "You see I'm quite partial to a fillet of male privilege with a side of entitlement." I cut a slice off the side of his belly and he cries out in pain. I try not to drop the slimy piece of meat, and lower it into my mouth. Just like chicken, but fattier in this case.

Colin's eyes roll back in his head and I wonder if he's losing consciousness already. It would make things a whole lot quieter. Nope, he's started screaming again. I might have to sit on his head in a minute. But first, I look up and down his body. So much to choose from. I slice off his nipple. His screams turn to squeals. The nipple is not very tasty. It's too grisly. He starts to thrash about so I straddle him, facing away from his face. I undo his belt and unzip his flies. I pull down his trousers and boxers just a little bit to expose his flaccid penis and hover my knife over the top.

"No, God no," Colin screams as I stare down at his pathetic shrivelled cock and wrinkly ball sack.

I contemplate for a moment. "Nah. I'd never be that hungry." I get up, grab his hair, or what's left of it, pull his head back and slice his neck from ear to ear. Blood gushes out all over the kitchen and I drop the knife. I stare at my hands and start licking the blood off my fingers. It's then that I notice the sandwich on the floor. All that creamy mayonnaise. I snatch it up and take a massive bite, and another, and another. The blood from my hands covers the sandwich but I keep eating and eating until it's all gone.

I rinse out my Tupperware tub and consider which bits of Colin I might want to take home for dinner, but the blood and shrivelled cock is a little off-putting.

"Fuck this," I say to myself. "I'm going to get pizza."

~

## Mel Ciavucco's Biography

Mel Ciavucco is a freelance writer from the UK. She is a blogger, fiction writer, screenwriter, editor and vlogger.

Mel is passionate about writing stories that challenge social norms, showcase diverse characters and contain realistic portrayals of mental health. She believes that sharing our stories and stepping out of our comfort zones makes us all better human beings.

She writes about body positivity and gender equality on her personal blog: www.melciavucco.weebly.com

Twitter: @MCiavucco

Facebook: www.facebook.com/melciavuccowriter

Instagram: www.instagram.com/melciavucco

~

# Mel's Competition Judging Comments

Another year, another wonderful 20 shortlisted stories. I always look forward to judging To Hull And Back. Such a range of stories – you never know what you're going to get, but the standard is always high.

It amazes me how humour can be translated in so many different ways, from subtle amusement to laugh out loud one-liners. This year, I especially enjoyed the heart-felt stories with underlying tones of humour. It's a real accomplishment to be able to make a reader laugh and cry in the same story.

Thank you and congratulations to all the shortlisted writers, and to Chris for continuing to run the most awesome short story writing competition in the world.

# SKYDIVING

*Judge's story, by Mark Rutterford*

If I were a skydiver, I would live for the moment when I stepped out of the plane, to free fall to the Earth and never be the same again. The exhilaration, the noise, the feeling sick, the wideness of my eyes and the G-force on my face, the adrenaline, the trouser filling fear – bring it on.

All of that and the shedding of inhibition and reality, so that I could be a different man.

I would float – well, dive – at 400 miles an hour, like a hawk, like a superhero. Many wouldn't, I would, and

I'd do it for myself, not to impress you. I'd do it because I had to, because not doing it was worse than doing it and dying an inglorious death, impaled on a fence post in the fields of England, with my balls hanging off a barb of barbed wire, somewhat shrivelled – cos it was cold up there – and dangling for all to see.

That's what it's like.

Falling in love.

I remember.

I remember Sally. She had freckles and white socks and sandals and dirty knees, all of which was alright, because she and I were only six. So, it wasn't really skydiving, it was more like being on the swings or the seesaw or the feeling when you spin around and around until you're dizzy and you fall to the grass and look up at the sky.

I felt the same way about my first football boots. But then you never forget your first love.

I stepped out of a plane once for Marie. I was thirteen and she was quatorze, on account of being French and a year older than me. It was one of those jumps where you sailed to the Earth in sunlight and without the need to open your parachute. One of those jumps where you landed on a carpet of snowdrops without breaking a petal. You didn't weigh anything at all, because you had just had your first kiss *with tongues*. Oh Marie, *Marie* – je t'aime alright. A bit wet and garlicky if I'm honest, but it was definitely t'aime and I was definitely feeling it.

A few years later and Sarah and I were so in love, we were invincible. Who isn't invincible at 17, right? Loved up and trusting enough to try out oral sex and not flinching at the pause required to take a pube out from between your teeth.

A few years after that and it was Wendy, a friend of my aunty that caught my attention. And I caught hers. She was 34, when I was 22. She was a Venus, I was a fly; happy to be trapped, I remember, but even then, my memory was selective.

I forgot that she was married and lived in a detached house, with two dogs (one of which was obviously her husband) and that she worked as a solicitor and was a proper grownup. I forgot I was barely a man, without a clear idea of what I was going to do with my life. I forgot the difference between dreaming and dreams coming true. It was a hard lesson to learn, but my balls were full of testosterone, so I seemed to bounce back.

20 years on and I was 10 years into a relationship that was as fragile as Donald Trump's membership of the Women's Institute. So, when JJ and I found ourselves on a shoot together, in the countryside of Bulgaria of all places, it was just another film. When we smiled at each other and chatted in the queue for lunch, it was evident that there was chemistry. We did what lots of attached people do when they are attracted to each other; we remembered we were attached and denied what we were feeling.

We remembered to call home each night. JJ remembered to call Louisiana and I remembered to call Lewisham. We remembered to send all our love and we forgot that our hearts were already cheating.

We bantered, JJ and I. She said a sound recordist was the most boring role on a shoot and that artistes, like her, were the ones that got the Oscars. I said I didn't give a flying fuck about her condescension and that stars and soundmen alike got the Bulgarian shits; there had been an outbreak on the set and it had put us behind schedule. JJ laughed and I forgot that I was a technician and she was a film star.

I took her to my sound van, to demonstrate my craft. I put a microphone on her wrist, so she could hear the beat of her pulse. Then I put it to her neck, so she could hear her jugular drumming away and feeding her brain. She looked focused, whilst I looked at the detail of her eyelashes and the curl of her mouth and the underside of her chin. I could trace the outline of her neck and I could smell the scent of her. She looked at me looking and, after a moment lost in her huge brown eyes, I blushed like a schoolgirl. Then I directed the mic to JJ's chest and I sang a song to the beat of her heart. We shared the headset and sat so close together that the mic would have picked up my heartbeat too... except it wasn't there. My heart was putting on a parachute and preparing for take-off.

JJ kissed me.

I forgot who I was and I kissed her back.

Then she remembered who she was and ran away like a startled racoon.

I remembered what it was like to be 6 and 17 and 22. And I was dizzy and invincible and forgetful that it could never work. And I remembered I was attached and JJ was married and an actress and lived in LA. So, for a week, we were professional and cordial and fake.

Except my heart, which had fuelled the engines and was cleared for take-off and had stowed away on the aircraft from which it was about to jump out. Excited and nauseous and true.

It remembered who I used to be and forgot who I was.

I blurted. A bit of a speech about how I had run a lot and beat myself with birch twigs after bathing in the river every morning, all to try and forget that I knew what I felt and that it was annoyingly life-changing. I apologised profusely and explained how I hated myself for it but, the fact was, I was a boring technician and although JJ was lovely and kind and the fantasy of a million men around the world, I had probably fallen for the sound of her wrist. I declared that my heart had remembered what this was and what this was... was serious. I felt sick and I jumped.

I can't deny... there was sex. I can't deny... it was great. And we got to know each other a lot in the space of those few weeks in Bulgaria. It was cocooned, I know. Emotional and exciting. Isolated and special. Not so much another country as another world. But the shoot ended and after soul-searching, many tears and a farewell hug that lasted 6 hours and 37 minutes before JJ's alarm went off, we parted. It was because JJ remembered that real life was a lot harder than in the movies and she wasn't sure enough that we could cope with it.

So, I forgot who I used to be and remembered who I was. I remembered that I wasn't the kind of man who was brave enough to go back to England and leave his partner. Not even for a famous actress, who would have to leave her famous husband to be with me. I remembered that I wasn't the kind of man who could maintain JJ's interest and I would always suspect she was destined to get bored of me and marry a superstar. I forgot that I wasn't man enough to go for it, not even for love.

So, I lost two stone with worry and guilt, then put three stones back on when my relationship broke up a year later. It was about then that I watched JJ and her husband at the Oscars.

I saw him look at her.

He was exhilarated and love-sick, with wide-eyes and G-force, with adrenaline... and with her.

I remembered what that felt like. To look at JJ that way. To sit close and smell her scent and hear the beating of her heart.

And I remembered, that there were no parachutes in Bulgaria.

And seeing her again brought back something I'd forgotten; the pain of being impaled on a fence-post, having fallen out of the sky.

~

## Mark Rutterford's Biography

Mark Rutterford is very confused. He doesn't know whether he is more writer or performer. If his emotions are more 13 year-old girl or a man raising his bat at reaching a half-century. Whether he should submit more for publication or for performance. If he should be focusing on short stories or novels. Whether he is a man or if he is an alien. So much a romantic it might be classified as a hidden-disability or whether that is his source of strength and inspiration.

So... Mark is all of these things, all at once – no wonder he is confused. To try and work things out, Mark writes and performs his stories around the South West of England.

Find out more on Mark's website:
www.markrutterford.com
Or chat on Twitter: @writingsett

~

# Mark's Competition Judging Comments

Humour – such a subjective thing. Humorous writing doubly so.

But this year I was reminded, in a rather lovely way, that humour is as diverse and as complex as any cross-section of the population – even if we call this sample a shortlist. Some laughs out loud, oh yes. Some wry smiles at precise observations that made my toes curl. Some quirky structures and themes and characters in some pretty unique circumstances too – bravo to them all. And some poignancy as well. I hadn't expected that – I liked it.

So huge thanks and many congratulations to all those who made the shortlist – what an achievement. It was a pleasure reading your work.

And huge thanks and a peerage to Lord Christopher Fielden... of Hull I presume.

# THE REAL MIRACLE

*Judge's story, by Mike Scott Thomson*

The first time Caitlin laid eyes on me, I was swallowing razor blades. She told me afterwards my performance had been so convincing, she'd taken out her mobile phone, pressed 9 and 9 again, and in the event I started vomiting scarlet parabolas of blood from an inadvertent but no less lethal hole in my gullet, she would press the third and final 9. Needless to say, that was entirely unnecessary and the razor blades came out one by one from between my lips, all threaded upon the length of cotton I had also swallowed. The audience rose to their feet, I took my bow and Caitlin and I started dating the very next week. I remember the first time I took her home and showed her around. The living room, the kitchen, the bathroom. When I got to the bedroom, I said, "This is where the magic happens." She laughed and flung her arms around me. Within three months, she'd moved in.

Three years later, I find myself standing outside our house, the one we bought together a year ago, trying my utmost to open the front door. It won't budge. It's clear she's finally followed through on her threat to kick me out and change the locks. I wiggle the key this way, that way, even try shoulder barging, but it won't move. The lock doesn't look different, but you know what locksmiths can do these days.

*So*, I think, *the magic has died*. Those blissful first few months when I would wake up with her sleeping peacefully by my side, and the sun would shine brighter through the curtains, and the first coffee of the day would have a deeper, earthier aroma than usual, and food would taste better, and the touch of her skin would send tiny electric shocks through my body. All of this. Dead.

All it took, it seems, was one late return home too many.

This evening, I swear, it was totally unplanned. For once, I wasn't going to work overtime at the estate agents or perform another magic show. I was going to make a real effort. "Fed up of it only being me in this relationship," she'd repeatedly tell me. It was only ever to be a very quick drink at Jimmy Bob's Wine Bar after work with Brian and Gav, and only because it was Gav's birthday. The last thing I expected was to bump into old Adam Cadabra.

Obviously, this was a stage name. To be quite honest, even as a 12-year-old when I first met him, I was never convinced of it. Adam Cadabra? For a magician? Really? But I looked up to him all the same. He was, after all, one of the foremost conjurers in the country: a member of the Associated Wizards of Great Britain with Golden Wand Honours. Thanks to a very generous birthday gift from my father, he was to be my mentor and tutor, helping me prepare my audition into that society's Southern Ring. As arranged, he arrived at our semi-detached house one Saturday morning. I answered the door and craned my neck up to him, a giant of a man, six foot six, with a craggy, Mount Rushmore face, black suit with red tie, and an alluring briefcase containing who-knows-what magical wonders. I still remember his first words to me.

"So, you're the little Paul Daniels." He smiled, just a brief smirk, and offered his hand for me to shake. It was smooth and strong; typical of a skilled manipulator. I was in awe.

He followed me upstairs to my bedroom where I kept all my tricks. For my audition, I had plans. I was going to conjure silk scarves from thin air, and from those scarves, I would produce lightbulbs – all lit – and then three of them would go floating and dancing over the heads of the audience, all in time to the music which, I decided, would be 'A Kind of Magic' by Queen. Then the lightbulbs would go floating back to me, and I would put them in a bag, one of those silky cloth sacks that magicians use, and all of them would turn into one gigantic crystal ball. The image of the Queen of Hearts would appear within it, and from that I would pluck a playing card from thin air – the same card, obviously – then, with a flick of the wrist, since it was the flick of the wrist wot did the trick, the card would morph into a bigger Queen, then a bigger one, then an even bigger one, then the card would be so big I'd be able to fold it into a box, out of which – POW – a real, living, breathing Queen of Hearts would emerge (my nine year old sister, who'd tentatively agreed, only after I bribed her with my pudding one evening), and I would take a huge bow, and I'd be the greatest magician who ever lived.

Quite how I was going to do all this was mere detail I would figure out in due course.

Anyhow, once I'd told Adam Cadabra about my extravaganza extraordinaire, he shuffled upon my chair, raised a bushy eyebrow and smirked again. He glanced around my cupboards which were chock full with tricks and props my paper round money had been able to afford. Finally, he spoke. "Less is more," he said, as if that were all there was to it. "Less is more." He clicked open his briefcase. My heart sank when all he retrieved was a sheet of A4 paper and a biro.

We decided on a routine where I would take a walking cane, make it float about a bit in time to 'Oxygene' by Jean Michel Jarre, morph it into two flowing red and white silk scarves, then take a blue one, magically blend those three silk scarves into the Union Flag, but 'accidentally' drop one beforehand so the flag ends up without any blue in it, so it looks like the trick went wrong. Then I would pretend to be confused ("You need to learn to be an actor," Adam told me), retrieve the blue silk from the floor, then conjure the flag as it should be. The end. The whole thing would take less than five minutes. "Less is more," he said once again as he handed me the notes he'd written. "Promise me you'll practice that?" I nodded. "And practice and practice some more?" I nodded, not sure whether to be star struck or disappointed. "Good lad." And then he left.

Anyway, I passed the audition – there were only 11 people in the audience – but it did the trick, no pun intended, since they admitted me as the youngest member of the society and, 20 years later, I'm still there.

Adam Cadabra, however, must have had bigger fish to fry because I never saw him again. Until, that is, just a couple of hours ago, in Jimmy Bob's, hunched over the bar, his large frame perched awkwardly on a barstool. I excused myself from Brian and Gav and sauntered over. "Hello?"

He slowly turned his head from his whiskey sour and looked up. Even after all these years, he was as imposing as ever, but now his face was more lined, small furrows through his forehead and jowls, and what had once been a Brylcreemed shock of brown hair was now dishevelled, dryer and grey.

"Mr... er... Cadabra?"

His once-bushy eyebrows shot up. I froze, wondering if I'd said the wrong thing. After a few seconds he turned back to his whiskey sour, raised it to his lips, downed it, then looked back at me. His misty blue eyes met mine.

"The little Paul Daniels," he murmured. I smiled, relieved. Adam hiccupped and raised his hand, not at me, but the barman. Five seconds later another whiskey sour appeared, as if by magic. "Lightbulbs and the Queen of Hearts," he drawled, pricks of sweat appearing on his brow. "Hocus Pocus, piff paff pouf."

And he fell off his stool. It was one of those moments, those utterly unaccountable, unpredictable instances, where one thinks, I have *no* information about this. No life experience whatsoever about what to do or what to think in such a situation. Like the time I realised one of my magic tricks had gone so disastrously wrong it would end up with my willing audience volunteer getting soaked with warm, soapy water. Adam's succumbing to gravity was one of those occasions. One of the foremost magicians in the country – or at least, at one time in the distant past – sprawled on the sticky tiles of a cocktail bar, his back on the floor, limbs pointing in the four directions of the compass.

It took me a second or two to respond. "Oh, Jesus Christ, Adam, are you OK?"

From out of nowhere Brian and Gav appeared. "Blimey, Mark, what did you do to him?" The two of them bent down and took an arm each, raising Adam's considerable frame to a more vertical position with surprising ease. Adam, for his part, didn't seem to mind – he'd started singing a song about the birds and the bees.

"Here," I said, guiding him towards a sofa. "Sit on something more comfortable."

Adam stopped singing as he sat down. "Magic is real, you know," he said. "What YOU do," he slurred pointing a shaking finger at me, "and what I USED to do, is trickery. Magic is reeeeeeeeeel." He drew out the word like my razor blades on a length of thread.

"Sure it is," I said.

He looked at me, a wave of sobriety clouding his face. "It IS real, because once it's GONE," he thumped his fist on the table as he raised his voice, "it's gone." He put his large hand to his chest. "Annabel," he said. "I made her disappear. Now I want the pain to disappear too." He looked down at an empty cocktail glass. "And I can no longer be an actor..."

"It's always a woman," whispered either Brian or Gav to the other. I shushed at them to be quiet.

Adam turned back to me. "My lad. D'ya have a woman?" I nodded. "Is she pretty?" I nodded again. "Less is more," he said, shaking his head. "Less of the gone time and more of the she time." He hiccupped again and scrunched his face.

Oddly, I understood his mangled attempts at communication. I had indeed been gone too often this past year. Working late at the office, putting in the occasional – oh, OK – frequent cabaret show. We had a new mortgage to pay. Could Caitlin not understand this?

Adam obviously had taken my private musings for doubt at his words. "Watch this," he said. Somehow or another, he'd got hold of my house keys. They must have fallen out of my coat pocket. Either that, or he'd picked me. He held up a Chubb key, no more than two inches in front of his nose.

"Hey fuckin' PRESTO," he yelled, making the other three of us jump. The key did nothing as Adam's face broke into hysterics. He fell back into the plump cushions of the armchair and yawned, showing two rows of yellow teeth.

"That's enough now," said the barman, who'd appeared from thin air, like the shopkeeper from Mr Benn. "Come on, Mr Fitzgerald. You've had enough for tonight."

Adam didn't complain. Clearly this rigmarole was routine. He rose to his feet, wobbling only slightly. He didn't even turn back as he broke into song, Perry Como's 'Magic Moments' this time, as he staggered across the lounge and out the door.

A few seconds silence passed, then I turned to Brian

and Gav. "My mentor," I explained. "He taught me everything I know."

I stayed another 30 minutes and had one orange juice – I promise, that was all – and now I'm back home, and I can't get in. I've tried calling Caitlin, but both her mobile and the landline just keep ringing. I wish I'd learned David Copperfield's 'Walking Through Walls' trick. Then I might be getting somewhere.

*God damn it*, I think. *She really has locked me out for good.* Just for luck, I barge the door one more time, when the world spins 180 degrees and I end up sprawled on the hallway floor, my face nestled between a pair of pink ladies' slippers. Caitlin is looming over me, having opened the door the same moment as my shoulder barge, her hair wet and bedraggled down to her waist, a fluffy bath towel protecting her modesty.

She presses her slippered feet upwards into my chin. "So there you are," she mutters. "Pissed again, I see?"

I need to explain fast. "No, no, no. Not drunk, but I was held up, I promise..." Caitlin puts her hands on her hips, waiting for the excuse this time. "I bumped into a very old friend, which was really bizarre, then came straight home but I couldn't get in." I scramble to my feet. "Look, the door wouldn't open."

"So I heard," she says. Maybe I've got away with it after all. Caitlin sidles past me to the door, now on its latch, and examines the lock. "Give me your keys."

"Here." I hand them over.

She tsks. "What *have* you been doing with them?" She holds up the Chubb key. It's bent along its shaft by at least 30 degrees. "No wonder it didn't work. You clumsy clod. Now we'll have to spend money we don't have getting a new one cut..." She shuffles off, back up the stairs, to the bathroom.

I examine the key. *Adam*, I think. *You crafty old jester.* I think of him, that towering, stone-faced old conjurer. My mentor.

Then I think of my lady. She's still here. Still with me. The real Queen of Hearts. No sleight-of-hand, trickery or misdirection required. That's the real miracle.

I click the front door shut and follow her upstairs.

~

## Mike Scott Thomson's Biography

Mike Scott Thomson has been a writer of fiction-on-the-shorter-side since 2011. Before that, he dallied with travel writing, blogs, and commissioned biographies of various popular beat combos. (In a gloriously random turn of events, these then became commercially available as audiobooks.)

His short stories have appeared in various publications such as *The Fiction Desk, Prole, Litro, Stories for Homes*, and an anthology from the National Flash Fiction Day.

Competition wins or placings include those from Inktears, Writers' Village, Momaya Press, and Chris's own To Hull And Back competition in its inaugural year. (His avatar still sits proudly upon the Hog of issue 1.) He now wants to give fiction-on-the-longer-side a go, and this time actually finish something.

Website: www.mikescottthomson.com
Twitter: @michaelsthomson

~

# Mike's Competition Judging Comments

Summing up this year's selection has been the hardest yet; the standard really has been that good. That said, once I'd read them and re-read them, I was happy with my own rankings of the stories. It has reaffirmed in my own mind a couple of the criteria I look for to be entertained by a morsel of specifically comic fiction.

Firstly, is the story told through a straight face? To my mind, humour works best when it doesn't seem to be trying too hard.

Secondly, does the story still work if the reader doesn't find it funny? A story that hinges too much upon gags, or a punchline, runs somewhat at a risk. Personally, there were some yarns in the selection which didn't tickle either of my funny bones, but I still ranked those highly as they were nonetheless brilliantly told.

All in all, being involved in To Hull And Back again has given me another timely reminder that opinions of all artful things are just that – opinions. Something I'll do well to remember next time any of my own efforts ends up closer to a recycling bin than a shortlist.

Congratulations to the winner: welcome to The Hog Hall of Fame.

# A FINAL NOTE

Thank you to all the writers who entered the competition and everyone that purchases this anthology. Your continued support allows this competition to grow and bring more attention to humorous writing.

While you wait for next year's anthology, why not take part in my writing challenges? They're all free to enter, every submission is published and money from book sales are donated to charity. Check them out here: www.christopherfielden.com/writing-challenges/

Until next year ☺

Chris Fielden

20576568R00145

Printed in Great Britain
by Amazon